THE GREAT FRUSTRATION

5·11

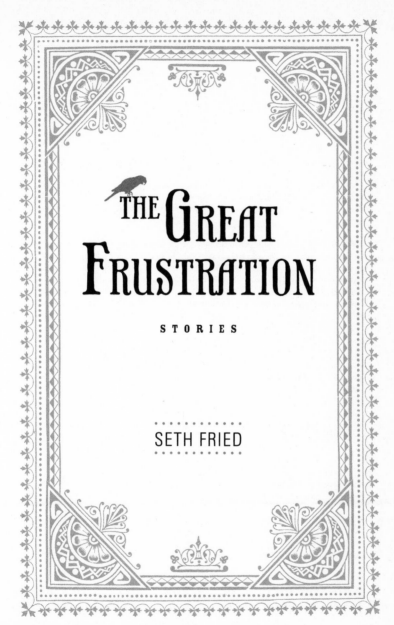

THE GREAT FRUSTRATION

STORIES

SETH FRIED

SOFT SKULL PRESS

AN IMPRINT OF COUNTERPOINT | BERKELEY

The following stories have been previously published, some in different forms: "Loeka Discovered" and "The Siege" in *The Missouri Review*; "Frost Mountain Picnic Massacre" in *One Story*, *Pushcart Prize XXXV: Best of the Small Presses*, and *The Year's Best Dark Fantasy & Horror 2010*; "Life in the Harem" in *Tin House*; "Those of Us in Plaid" in *McSweeney's*; "Lie Down and Die" in *McSweeney's* and *The Better of McSweeney's, Volume 2*; "The Misery of the Conquistador" in *StoryQuarterly*; Excerpts from "Animalcula: A Young Scientist's Guide to New Creatures" in *JMWW*, *The Kenyon Review*, and *Ninth Letter*.

Library of Congress Cataloging-in-Publication Data is available

Fried, Seth.
  The great frustration : stories / Seth Fried.
    p. cm.
  ISBN 978-1-59376-416-6
  I. Title.
  PS3606.R5525G74 2011
  813'.6—dc22
                        2011005452

Cover design by Anna Bauer
Interior design by Elyse Strongin, Neuwirth & Associates, Inc.
Printed in the United States of America

Soft Skull Press
An imprint of Counterpoint
1919 Fifth Street
Berkeley, CA 94710

www.softskullpress.com | www.counterpointpress.com

Distributed by Publishers Group West

10 9 8 7 6 5 4 3 2 1

CONTENTS

Loeka Discovered   1

Frost Mountain Picnic Massacre   25

Life in the Harem   43

Those of Us in Plaid   63

The Misery of the Conquistador   73

The Great Frustration   85

The Siege   93

The Frenchman   107

Lie Down and Die   115

The Scribes' Lament   119

Animalcula: A Young Scientist's Guide to New Creatures   135

LOEKA DISCOVERED

· · · · · · · · · · ·

Whether or not it had been his intention to impress anyone, Loeka, the lab favorite, had managed to climb four thousand feet without modern mountain-climbing equipment—and those of us on the research team had to admit that was pretty damned impressive. Objectivity is important, but we liked Loeka. What was the matter with that? The ice had kept him in good shape for more than seven thousand years, and in his wrenched-up face the flesh was warped into an excruciating grimace. The pathos of the whole thing was unshakable. After our third day of working on Loeka, Doc Johnson (who was somewhat of a relic himself and who until then hadn't shown more than an ounce of emotion in his forty years as Director at the Institute) started the day by reading aloud from a poem he had written about Loeka. The poem focused on what were presumed to be his last moments, shivering on the mountainside. In the poem, Loeka is determined to get back to his family but is too weak to move. In the end, he looks up at the stars and feels warmed by their distant light. His last thoughts are of the fate of his poor family, huddled together in some primitive, thatch-roofed dwelling. He bravely attempts to stand and keels forward, taking on the prone, abject pose in which he was found by Norwegian tourists more than a half dozen millennia later.

The poem wasn't very good. It rhymed too much, and Doc Johnson's voice warbled in a way that made us feel uncomfortable. However, most of us were still somewhat touched. We watched Doc Johnson's hands shake a little more than usual as he folded the sheet of notebook paper with his poem on it and returned it to the pocket of his lab coat. Gathered in a circle, our eyes misty, we began to get the sensation, a swelling in our chests, that what we were working on was important—that it was bigger than all of us.

There was something spellbinding about it, peering down the vast well of time at Loeka's small, puckered face. While extracting a tissue sample for analysis, it wasn't uncommon for any one of us to sing to Loeka sweetly or to talk to him as if he were an obedient child. Whereas before we would march down the sterile, artificially lit halls of the Institute, nodding to one another as we passed, the air around us a cold flutter of clipboards and clicking pens, we now began to stop and greet one another, laughing. Two weeks with Loeka, and some of the men started showing up to the lab in more brightly colored shirts and gag neckties. Some of the women traded their slacks for skirts that ended just below the knee, traded their sensible loafers for something with a heel; their vibrant clacks echoed down the corridors, which, once gray and subdued, now seemed charged with untold possibility.

Every day there were more newspapers and magazines clamoring for interviews about Loeka. We tried to be as calm and plainspoken as possible, but the fervor of the moment quickly overtook us. We delivered our interviews breathlessly to an unending bank of microphones. Yes, his leather boots were being developed commercially. Yes, they were surprisingly comfortable. No, his axe was made of copper. Yes! Yes! We gave the reporters large, toothy grins and finished one another's sentences. We winked wryly at one another when a question was broad or obvious. When leaving the interviews, we took one another by the arm, walking back to our posts with a sense of privilege, a kind of giddiness.

There was an excitement building in us. The isotopic analysis of his tooth enamel, as well as the paleodontal staining, determined Loeka's point of origin to be a small village in northern Italy near modern-day Vahrn, some three hundred miles from the place of his discovery. We marveled: what could have caused him to travel so far, so high? Geological records confirmed that at the time of Loeka's death, his native region would have been in the throes of a prolonged drought. This, combined with the fact that we found no processed grains in Loeka's digestive tract, only conifers and berries, suggested that he was most likely a type of scout, heading out into dangerous, unknown lands to find a place more livable for his drought-wracked village. Instantly, Loeka was miraculous and selfless. Loeka was endeavor.

Somewhere in the lab a machine would whir and clap and we would draw our faces in close, waiting for the results. Our hot, eager breath clouding the film of some X-ray, we would imagine Loeka swaggering up the mountainside with savage bravado, mumbling softly to himself in some ancient tongue as the dangers increased, "I'll think of *something*."

It's no surprise that small romances began to bubble up throughout the lab. At the time, it seemed to make sense. It wasn't long before our working in such close proximity, together with the general excitement of the task at hand, led to lingering glances over calorimeters, colleagues leaning in to share the dual eyepieces on comparison microscopes, the sudden, accidental brush of hands simultaneously attempting to adjust the needle valves of Bunsen burners. When we examined some of the pollen we found in Loeka's colon, it turned out that the cells within the pollen were still intact, which meant that Loeka's death could be placed sometime during the spring. Spring! Even Doc Johnson developed a somewhat platonic crush on Laurel, one of our interns. His eyes would follow her longingly across the lab as she shuffled papers or fetched a pair of forceps or, engrossed in some menial task and feeling unwatched, blew a distracted puff of breath through her dark, lovely bangs. Doc Johnson seemed afflicted but happy, and his old, soft leather briefcase bulged with what we could only assume to be an outpouring of new, unreadable poems, which had most likely been written, in some harmless sense, for Laurel.

The lab was alive with a strange new confidence. We all moved with a rakish strut, our clothing slightly disheveled. Some of us high-fived and slapped backsides. Others adopted nicknames. Dr. O'Reilly started calling himself "the Clipper." Dr. Clifford and Dr. Simmons demanded that we refer to them as "Scooter" and "Long Shot," respectively. Dr. Stevens insisted that we call him "Big Tex," despite the fact he was only 5'6" and from Maryland.

The subtle flirtations in the lab grew into white-hot animal compulsions. We attacked one another's blouse buttons and pant zippers in storage closets, revealing surprisingly taut, youthful bodies long obscured by baggy clothing and the horrible fog of professionalism. Those of us who were married came home early, sending our bewildered children to their rooms long before their usual bedtime. We took our husbands and wives wherever we found them, in a loud clamor of unwashed pots, TV trays, and laundry baskets. We scratched and pulled toward one another madly. Laurel began wearing ribbons in her hair, and one bright afternoon Doc Johnson sauntered into the lab wearing a pair of white shorts and a striped boatneck.

We fell into our research as if it were the most lurid, tempting thing of all. We performed simple tasks diligently and with a heightened sense of responsibility. Our minds raced. When faced with various disjointed segments of data, complex mental associations on our part, precise leaps of intuition, and all-out breakthroughs were immediate and common. It was a pace that was not easily contained. During an idle moment, many of us would take the opportunity to scribble in the margins of our notepads ideas for the types of personal projects that hadn't haunted our private ambitions in years. Rushing between tasks, we would write the titles of possible articles on coffee-stained napkins, quickly folding them into our pockets. We drummed our fingers while we worked, thinking about the world in terms of problems and philosophies of improvement. There was a creative mania spreading everywhere, a contagious energy which, though intoxicating, never distracted us from our primary task: Loeka. We threw ourselves passionately into our investigation. We pursued it with the utmost care and fastidiousness, as even the simplest procedure had become for us a deliberate act of celebration as well as a rejection of the pessimism and doubt that we felt had characterized our lives up to that point.

Every morning we wrote out affirmations in the steam on our bathroom mirrors, sang with the radios in our cars. The world was new. Everything flew forward. One discovery unfolded into two, three, several. Laurel's youth and beauty descended over the lab like a cloud. Doc Johnson's heart rang out. In his eyes we could see the first cannon shot, the first launched ship, the first cry of victory and defeat. The world was ancient.

Some nights we threw impromptu parties on the roof of the Institute. We would watch the stars, wondering how they might have looked to Loeka some seven thousand years ago. Drinking champagne, we would laugh and lift our glasses. Drunker and drunker, we toasted in unison: "Loeka! Loeka!" We kept it up for as long as our voices held out, the toast becoming steadily louder and more jubilant —"Loeka! Loeka!"— until the name itself grew shorter, its vowels and consonants softer, eventually sounding, perhaps not coincidentally, something like "Life!"

Then they found the Big Man.

Just as our research was achieving new heights, a call came in about another body. On the same mountain where Loeka had been discovered, another natural mummy was uncovered several hundred feet higher. The Big Man, so named immediately due to his large frame, which early reports remarked as being intimidating even in death, was found, ironically, because of the attention the area had received as a result of the publicity surrounding Loeka. While we first expected something similar to Loeka (a thought which intrigued us) the initial photographs emailed to us at the Institute were not promising. Unlike Loeka's small, endearing face, with its features lumpy and vague like something molded roughly out of clay, the face of the Big Man was freakishly well preserved and hideous. With a prominent forehead, sunken eyes, and smashed-in nose, he had the look of something alien, violent and unfriendly. Most of us were put off by the photographs but easily recovered. Charged by the notion of a new specimen and all its mysteries, we cheered. We banged on the tube of the MRI machine, shouting in to Loeka over the sound of the Eric Clapton we pumped in sort of as a joke, as if to prevent him from being frightened by the incessant knocking sound produced by the machine. We hollered into the tube stupidly, telling Loeka, "You're going to have a friend!"

Within days of the discovery, the Big Man was shipped to the Institute in a large, pressurized crate. Our playfulness over the idea of another mummy had subsided, and for the first few hours following the Big Man's arrival we managed only to stare at the crate uncertainly. Most of us seemed to feel an uneasiness with respect to the Big Man and a desire to return our attention to Loeka. Our interest in the Big Man as an abstract idea quickly gave way to defensiveness the moment he became a physical presence in the lab, as if the existence of the Big Man were somehow an affront to Loeka. Half the morning was spent in silence before Doc Johnson shuffled up to the crate and punched in the nine-digit passcode, upon which the crate opened with a slow and unsettling hiss.

We were anxious to see what we might be able to learn from the Big Man, but something about him had cast a shadow over our research. We managed to establish him as contemporaneous to Loeka, and we initiated the analysis of his tooth enamel, but tasks that had only recently seemed to perform themselves—so ecstatically involved were we in their execution—now seemed insufferable. One of us would return from a remote testing facility with a fresh printout, and all activity in the lab would stop. "Well," someone would ask, "what does it say?" At which point whichever one of us had fetched the data would hold the paper uncomfortably, as if unsure which way to turn it, eventually saying, "I don't know."

The reaction from the press was marked with a curiosity that was similar to that with which they had received Loeka. However, their overall excitement was diminished. Even the sharp slaps of their flashing cameras were somehow less urgent. The questions asked were quietly skeptical, as if the inability of the Big Man to surprise them after Loeka allowed the reporters to call into question the value of both discoveries. If the presence of the reporters had once delighted us, it now left us feeling a little upset, not only because we recognized that the press was fickle, that it was only able to judge the importance of things on their ability to awe and confound, but because, in terms of their misgivings and vague disinterest regarding the Big Man, we completely agreed with them.

It was not possible to approach the Big Man without first considering him in relation to Loeka; the differences between the two were staggering. Loeka's anguished look caused him to seem no longer as courageous in his frozen torment as we had first assumed. Observing him next to the Big Man, we had to admit that Loeka's expression suddenly appeared groveling and bullied, simply greedy for life.

In our minds, Loeka began to seem like a coward.

However, we did not find the brutish look of the Big Man more appealing. Rather, his impressive stature reminded us only of the incredible violence and cruelty of which humans were capable. While all that had been found in Loeka's digestive tract suggested the diet of a vegetarian, the Big Man's was packed with one continuous hank of red meat. The Big Man made clear how dangerous the past must have been, how easily someone like Loeka might have been exploited, how grim and pointless anyone's fate would have been, grunting, struggling in the dirt, if they were to have found themselves in the Big Man's hands.

The Big Man had carried with him a bow, along with a quiver of bone-tipped arrows. Attached to his belt were two knives and a small leather pouch filled with human teeth. His ears were notched in several places, and his forearms were heavily scarred. We were repulsed. When preparing the Big Man for any of the countless procedures that were required, we squinted in disgust and breathed through our mouths, as if we were bathing a vagrant. We found ourselves so over-whelmed by our dislike of the Big Man that if we dropped an instrument or stubbed our toe on the observation table, we had to restrain ourselves from taking out our anger on the Big Man's corpse or the surrounding equipment. We even had to fire an intern who, after a simple complication, swore at the Big Man and threw a scalpel at his forehead. An undergraduate from Brown named Kenny, he emptied out his workstation in a huff, stopping to look over the lab and declare briefly that the situation was "such total bullshit."

And while none of us had ever really liked that particular intern and had, in fact, been looking for a reason to let him go since the day he arrived, we still empathized with him. Though we would never admit it, many of us felt that the Big Man had it coming. When the airborne scalpel trembled to a stop in his forehead, many of us had even smiled approvingly. If anything, we found it touching that this young man who had paraded around the lab for seven months wearing the same Rolling Stones T-shirt and referring to all of us as "Dr. Dude" had sensed in his own vacuous way that the Big Man represented something awful. It had worked on his nerves as it had ours. In fact, he may have said it best. Though we couldn't put our fingers on it exactly, something about the Big Man *was* bullshit. However, Doc Johnson insisted on Kenny's dismissal, and in the end we were perfectly happy to see him leave. We watched him depart without comment and then returned our attention to our tests, our spreadsheets, our mummies, and our dwindling spirits.

Naturally, the air of romance in the lab diminished as well. As our enthusiasm for our work suffered, so did our attitudes toward our colleagues. We grew frustrated with each other. Those people in the lab who had excited us before—those with whom we had slipped off into storage closets for quick romps under fire blankets and between mop buckets, those who had only recently filled us with an unequivocal joie de vivre, our eyes meeting from across the lab, our laughter booming out together in the decontamination chambers—those same people began to bore us. Even Doc Johnson appeared to suspect something suddenly undesirable about Laurel. It was difficult to say what. Perhaps it was the way she pouted when Kenny was let go. Or perhaps it was that Doc felt her looks were finally too childish—those ribbons!—or that her shyness, which had appealed to him at first, was really just the conceited silence of a brat. Perhaps he imagined in her face something that was ready to age prematurely, something fat, stupid, and selfish. Whatever the case, his demeanor toward her changed entirely, and his briefcase slowly deflated.

We now regarded each other as almost poisonous. We saw our colleagues as robbing us of not only our creative potential but also our ability to complete the most basic tasks. They were parasites, demanding, with their idiotic pleasantries and mere presence in the lab, more than we were prepared to give. All their good ideas were just simple variations on our own. We found their work insipid and kept our own as closely guarded as possible. Although, once we succeeded in avoiding one another or in driving one another away with harsh words, we just as quickly turned on ourselves. Left alone, we began to see our work as obscure and self-indulgent. We wondered if the quality of our ideas was actually dependent on the ideas of those colleagues we had just driven away. We wondered if *we* were parasites. Had our relationships with our colleagues changed so quickly because of something latently flawed that they had recognized in us? We began to think that maybe there was nothing wrong with them at all but that we were just oblivious, emotionally handicapped monsters, doomed for the rest of our lives to commit the same sins against all the well-meaning people who would ever be unfortunate enough to find themselves in our paths.

Those of us who were married started working late, despite the fact that, as our interest in our work waned, there was less and less to be done. We ignored phone calls from our husbands and wives and pretended to fall asleep as soon as our heads hit the pillow. Our spouses, in turn, began to leave our suppers uncovered on kitchen tables, along with dejected notes, which, when read together over time, mapped out the course of their frustration and doubt.

We started keeping bottles of Beefeater and Jameson in our desks. Our hygiene suffered, and the lab took on the musty, alcoholic stink of a frat house. Whatever romances survived the mood of dissatisfaction that had swept through the lab were finally extinguished by embarrassing, alcohol-fuelled rendez-vous in the unisex bathrooms. Grinding their bodies together perfunctorily, unable to arouse one another, colleagues would fall asleep on stall floors with their pants undone, drooling on each other and gently breaking wind. We became moody and reckless. One afternoon, someone threw a portable mass spectrometer out of a third-story window into the parking lot. Three days later, Dr. Cukerski, our radiologist, was arrested after he came home drunk and proceeded to knock his wife around their condo for the two hours it took for the police to show up.

We looked awful. We felt awful. Doc Johnson stopped wearing his toupee for the first time in fifteen years. Men worked in the lab for days at a time with their flies down, women with the backs of their skirts tucked into their nylons.

It was in the grips of this melancholy that we finally knew whom to blame: Loeka.

Yes, our original distaste was for the Big Man, but as things progressed we realized that he was only a small part of how all the promise surrounding Loeka had turned up empty. Once a brave, lone man so far up a mountain, now he was only some prehistoric patsy with a sour look on his face. Why couldn't he have been alone on that mountain? Was that too much to ask? Why should something so simple and seemingly inspiring have to end up more complicated? It wasn't what anyone wanted.

Then we discovered the arrowhead.

There it was, on the X-ray, the size of a walnut, with a small taper of wooden shaft still attached, lodged under Loeka's right shoulder blade. Clear as day. Though we might have missed it if it weren't for the fact that some of the lab technicians had been using X-ray films as coasters. The film, stinking of stale booze, bore a small circle of water damage, enclosing the arrowhead perfectly and revealing to us by chance what would later seem obvious.

After the arrowhead's careful extraction, we confirmed that it was identical to the arrows carried in a large buckskin quiver by the Big Man. It was at almost the exact same moment that we received results of the analysis of the teeth that the Big Man carried in a small leather pouch on his belt. Having already characterized the Big Man as a simple brute, we assumed that his bag of teeth had been collected over a long campaign of violence spread out over a great distance. However, we were amazed to learn that these teeth, gathered from over forty different individuals, all responded to the paleodontal staining identically to the tooth sample we had taken from Loeka. These findings, paired with the results from the isotopic analysis, indicated that the teeth were all from the same point of origin, three hundred miles away and centered around a single population center near Vahrn, Loeka's village.

Stunned, we called for more tests. The Grayson came back positive. The Comparative Battery for Postdeciduous Tooth Matter scored in the ninety-eighth percentile. Laruth's reactant showed a bright orange. Everything pointed to Vahrn.

Having wandered down from the far north, the Big Man had apparently collected the teeth of over forty individuals from a single village, Loeka's village, in one unimaginable episode. For the first time in months our curiosity was piqued.

If the Big Man had murdered Loeka's entire village, it meant that Loeka, having somehow survived the attack, must have then pursued the Big Man over three hundred miles and up a mountain. The Big Man must have shot Loeka as he was pursued, before the two of them finally died in inclement weather, at high altitudes.

Loeka, willing to confront an extraordinary foe with only his diminutive stature and sad copper axe, was once again a hero—though not the hero we had at first envisioned. He was not some sensible man braving the understandable risks of nature in order to scout more suitable land for his people, but a man driven by the madness of an unbelievable loss, a man subject to a pain that must have been more than he could bear, a man less willing to sit still than to die.

Thousands of years later, there they were, frozen on a mountainside like the lovers on the Grecian urn, caught in eternal pursuit: Loeka pitched forward, gripping his axe, forever awaiting the delivered wound that would kill the Big Man or the wound received that would set him free.

Establishing an incredible precedent, several of the men in the lab shaved. Some of the women began combing their hair and applying lipstick, as, in a roundabout way, the practice of hygiene slowly snuck back into the lab. Doc Johnson began wearing a toupee again, but one much more modest than the old, towering bouffant he had once sported. His new hair was more closely fitted to the scalp. He didn't look as confident as he once had, but he now approached his age with some measure of acceptance; he walked through the lab in an attitude of slow determination and new maturity. Laurel received a bouquet of yellow roses, symbolizing both friendship and apology. In the absence of a card she assumed they were from Kenny, but we all knew who had actually sent them.

And while we felt that old enthusiasm returning, we knew that this time we had to accept our admiration of Loeka for what it was: a bias. We had to guide it, stay in front of it. We had to talk down to it, like a dog. We marched through the lab, all of us stern but invigorated. We spoke brusquely to one another, offering up only short, informative declarations.

"Here is a beaker."

"I have the results."

"My goggles are broken."

"You may borrow mine."

We felt properly jaded and able to go about the task at hand. Our former zeal appeared as childish as it did remote. Now, our resolve was intact. Our upper lips were stiff. Our brows, furrowed. We were unflinching and dispassionate. At last, we were true men and women of science.

Of course, Loeka still managed to charm us. With the new twist on his story, it was not unlike having an old friend back in the lab. But we recognized this impulse as the same type of foolishness that had led us to act irresponsibly in the first place. We discontinued that line of thought and returned our attention to discovering once and for all the secret of Loeka's death and the events that surrounded it. We were moving forward, setting out to prove beyond any reasonable doubt that the Big Man, though the logistics seemed incredible, had murdered Loeka's entire village and then been pursued by Loeka over a great distance. That was what had happened. It was our job to find out how.

The first thing we did was arrange another press conference. We were eager to see the looks on the reporters' faces when we showed them the arrow in Loeka's shoulder and the Big Man's bag of teeth. We even prepared an artistic rendering, which speculated what the Big Man's assault on Loeka's village might have looked like. Divided into twelve separate panels, the first pictured the Big Man slitting the throat of an elderly woman, while the second showed him smashing a man's head open on a sharp rock. In one panel, the Big Man was sodomizing a boy, already dead. In another, he was eating the flesh of a small girl, still alive. He was pictured strangling the villagers, hacking off their limbs, blinding them, mutilating their genitals, peeling long drapes of skin from their faces and chests and backs. Observing the sketch in all its gore, we knew that the press, which had once treated us so capriciously, would finally understand the magnitude of our work, the implications of our discovery.

And so, our suits crisp beneath our lab coats, we met the reporters who gathered.

We spoke with authority. We showed them the X-ray of Loeka's shoulder and the test results determining both the origin of the arrow and the bag of teeth. We spoke of these items in a manner that was both technical and detached.

However, when these facts failed to rouse the reporters, who listened to us in a way that was surprisingly indifferent, we took the opportunity to depart from what we strictly knew. We began to speak with enthusiasm about the Big Man's murderous rampage and Loeka's pursuit. We spoke about all the things, which, though they couldn't yet be proven, could easily be extrapolated from the facts of the case. We spoke excitedly, gesticulating wildly. We felt the muscles in our necks strain against our collars. We worked ourselves into such a frenzy that, once finished, we were almost startled. As if our minds, thousands of miles away and up a mountain, had suddenly come crashing back into the room of reporters—who now seemed more annoyed than anything. They picked their teeth and looked at their watches. Most of the photographers, tired of holding up their cameras, had set them at their feet. The only audible sounds in the room came from the whir of the ceiling fans, the drone and flicker of the fluorescent lights.

We tried to gain their interest. We tried desperately to keep all the energy in the room moving toward our single goal of impressing upon these reporters the importance of what was being said. When we finally unveiled our speculative sketch, the room burst into flat-out laughter. The reporters began to leave, shaking their heads in disbelief; some stopped to make catcalls and accuse us of bad taste. We tried to defend ourselves, but things got a little out of hand. A shouting match ensued, and in the confusion Big Tex was forced to wrestle to the ground a reporter from *The Washington Post*. Tex split the man's lip and then proceeded to chase a handful of reporters off into the parking lot.

The whole thing was a disaster. Nothing about Loeka made it to print, and two weeks later there was a picture in *National Geographic* of Tex flipping off a news van and pounding on its hood with his shoe. It was the first press conference we'd ever brought Laurel to, and the poor kid was pretty shook up. Doc Johnson found her crying underneath the dais, fished her out, and walked her back to the lab with his blazer over her shoulders.

We hung behind, listening to Tex's mad shouts from the parking lot and Laurel's sad little yelps from down the hall. We stood in the empty conference room, chairs toppled, notepads abandoned, speculative sketch torn asunder. It was enough to make one lose all hope. The only consoling thought was that we knew none of it was our fault.

In fact, we recognized our earlier efforts to be dispassionate as naive. Science was passion. If we wanted to prove something to be true, we had to act as if it already was. If we wanted to find three hundred uses for the peanut, we had to put the peanut to use. If we were being unreasonable, it was because science was unreasonable. We believed in Loeka. We believed that if we looked hard enough, we could prove what we felt we already knew.

The press conference had steeled our resolve. We set out to make use of every resource, to utilize every piece of evidence, to do whatever it took until our theory was borne out.

We called in an expert in terminal ballistics, Lt. Colonel John Munster, an older, well-groomed man in military dress. He listened to our presentation concerning the Big Man and Loeka attentively, though when it came time for him to examine the X-ray of Loeka's shoulder, he glanced at it only briefly before tossing it aside. With a smack of his lips, he posited rather glibly that the position of the arrow showed clearly that Loeka had been shot from behind. Furthermore, he said that the angle at which the arrow had entered his shoulder suggested that it had been fired not only from behind him, but from beneath him. Based on this evidence, he said it was far more likely that the Big Man had pursued Loeka up the mountain, shot him, and then moved on.

Munster was in surprisingly good shape for someone his age, and it took six of us to eject him from the lab.

Then, as if that weren't enough, one of our own turned on us. Dr. Albergotti, charged with the responsibility of analyzing the leather pouch containing the Big Man's collection of teeth, claimed to be able to prove with a high degree of certainty that the pouch had first belonged to Loeka, that the leatherwork was in keeping with the type produced in the area surrounding Loeka's point of origin. He said that this, in conjunction with the report of the ballistics expert, made it far more likely that the Big Man had simply taken the bag of teeth from Loeka after stumbling across him in the wild and murdering him for no apparent reason. He mentioned that in many forms of pagan worship, individuals gathered relics of their dead. He concluded that the fact that the bag contained so many teeth from so many different individuals of the same area and time period actually supported our earlier assumption that Loeka's village had been in the midst of a drought and possible famine at the time of his departure. When we asked him what a forensic scientist knew about pagan worship, he admitted rather sheepishly that he had Googled it.

Soon after that, some equipment went missing, and we had to let Albergotti go. It was nothing to involve the authorities over: some computer paper, a few staplers, a desk. There was no hard evidence to show that he took anything, but it was obvious to everyone that he was a dangerous element. We never did find that desk. After Albergotti was banned from the building, no one looked.

And while it was difficult to push forward, we did just that. We persevered. We worked thirty-two-hour shifts and didn't complain. We pored over everything again and again—but something was wrong. The harder we looked, the less we found. Elusive, the evidence contracted and folded in on itself. Before our very eyes, it disappeared. We struggled to find the linchpin in our argument, the one thing that would make everything come clear. And just as the fight was most desperate, just as our courage was cresting, just as we saw ourselves about to plummet headfirst into either total failure or the purest discovery, Doc Johnson had a stroke.

It was a terrible thing, not just for him but for the Institute. When we watched him collapse into that tray of beakers, we suddenly felt sapped of all our strength. As he was lying there, groaning on the floor, his lab coat flipped up over his head, we knew it would be his last day at the Institute.

He recovered somewhat. He confined himself to his home, not far from the Institute, where Laurel visited him every day, reading him the paper and keeping him updated on our progress back at the lab. After months of difficult rehabilitation he was talking again and writing. After a while longer he was walking and promising to be back in the lab again soon. Then he had four more strokes and died.

After that, everything happened at once. Members of the board came to inspect the Institute in the hopes of promoting someone among us to replace Doc Johnson as Director. However, there was some controversy when they found that in Doc Johnson's absence we had started drinking again—not to mention the fact that when they asked us to produce the Big Man, none of us could find him. After an extensive search, we found him in one of the break rooms, his head wedged behind a microwave. We were fired, of course. Loeka and the Big Man were relocated to a facility at Stanford, and even in light of all her hard work the board decided that Laurel would not receive any college credit for her efforts.

When the photographs of the Big Man as he had been found in the break room were released to the press, along with the photos of us weeping in the parking lot as they took Loeka away, we had our fair share of embarrassment. Also, Dr. Redding from the Stanford program managed to get in a few shots at us on *The Charlie Rose Show*. But afterward it wasn't difficult for any one of us to get a job teaching at some community college or working in a commercial lab, which can be pleasant enough. Sure, Dr. Redding would probably have something sharp to say about that, but it's really not that bad. Occasionally some small reminder will make us cringe. The outline of a tooth on a dentist's window. A picture of a mountain. A small man on the street with a pained look on his face. Though just as often, we'll see the stars at night and wonder once again how they might have looked to Loeka. We'll try to remind ourselves that despite everything, we had believed in something. And what was the matter with that?

FROST MOUNTAIN PICNIC MASSACRE

. . . .

Last year, the people in charge of the picnic blew us up. Every year it gets worse. That is, more people die. The Frost Mountain Picnic has always been a matter of uncertainty in our town and the massacre is the worst part. Even the people whose picnic blankets were not laid out directly upon the bombline were knocked unconscious by the airborne limbs of their neighbors, or at least had the black earth at the foot of Frost Mountain driven under their eyelids and fingernails and up into their sinuses. The apple dumpling carts and cotton candy stands and guess-your-weight booths that were not obliterated in the initial blasts leaned slowly into the new-formed craters, each settling with a limp, hollow crumple. The few people along the bombline who survived the blast were at the very least blown into the trees.

The year before that, the boom of the polka band had obscured the scattered reports of far-off rifles. A grown man about to bite a caramel apple suddenly spun around wildly, as if propelled by the thin spray of blood from his neck. An old woman, holding her stomach, stumbled into a group of laughing teenagers. Someone fell forward into his funnel cake and all day long we walked around as if we weren't aware of what was happening.

One year, the muskets of the Revolutionary War Reenactment Society were somehow packed with live ammunition. Another year, all the children who played in the picnic's Bouncy Castle died of radiation poisoning. Yet another year, it was discovered halfway through the picnic that a third of the port-a-potties contained poisonous snakes. The year that the picnic offered free hot air balloon rides, none of the balloons that left—containing people laughing and waving from the baskets, snapping pictures as they ascended—ever returned.

Nevertheless, every year we still turn out in the hundreds to the quaint river quay in our marina district to await the boats that will take us to Frost Mountain. In a hilltop parking lot, we apply sunscreen to the noses of our children. We rifle through large canvas carryalls, taking inventory of fruit snacks, extra jelly sandals, Band-Aids, and juice boxes, trying to anticipate our children's inevitable needs and restlessness in the twenty minutes that they will have to wait for the boats to be readied. Anxious to claim our place in line, we head down the hill in a rush toward the massive white boats aloft in the water.

We wait in a long, roped queue that doubles back on itself countless times before reaching the loading platform with its blue vinyl awning. Once it's time to depart, the line will move forward, leading us to the platform, where the deckhands will divide us up evenly among the various boats. From there, we will be moved upriver, to the north of our city, where Frost Mountain looms. From the decks, we will eventually see a lush, green field interrupted by brightly colored tents and flashing carnival rides, the whole scene contained by the incredible height of Frost Mountain, reaching into the sky with its cold, blue splendor.

The sight of the picnic at the foot of Frost Mountain is so appealing that most of us will, once again, convince ourselves that this year will be different, that all we have in store for us is a day full of leisure and amusements—but sooner or later, one of the rides will collapse, or a truck of propane will explode near one of the food tents, killing dozens.

Of course, every year more people say they won't come. Every year, there are town meetings during which we all condemn the Frost Mountain Picnic. We meet in the empty tennis courts of the Constituent Metro Park where we vow to forsake the free bags of peanuts, the free baked butternut squashes, the free beer, the free tractor rides and firework expositions.

We grow red in the face, swearing our eternal alignment against all the various committees, public offices, and obscure private interests in charge of organizing the picnic. Every year, there are more people at the meetings who are walking on crutches and wearing eye patches from the injuries they sustained the previous year. Every year, there are more people holding up pictures of dead loved ones and beating their chests. Every year, there are more people getting angry, interrupting one another, and asking the gathered crowd if they might be allowed to speak first. Every year, loyalty oaths are signed. Every year, pledges to abstain from the Frost Mountain Picnic are given and received freely and every single year, without exception, everyone ends up going to the picnic anyway.

Often, the people who are the most vocally opposed to the picnic are also the most eager to get there, the people most likely to cut in line for the boats, the people most disdainful toward the half-dozen zealots picketing in the parking lot.

Waiting in line for the boats, our children rub their chins in the dirt and push their foreheads against our feet. They roll around on the ground and shout obscenities, then run in circles, screaming nonsense, while we play with the car keys in our pockets and gawk passively at the boats. Typically, we don't allow our children to misbehave this way. However, we do our best to understand. Their faces are in pain.

Our children's cheeks begin to ache as they wait in line for the boats and continue to ache until their faces are painted at the Frost Mountain Picnic. We've come to understand that all children are born with phantom cat whiskers. All children are born with phantom dog faces. All children are born with phantom American flag foreheads, rainbow-patterned jawbones, and deep, curving pirate scars, the absence of which haunts them throughout their youth. We understand that all children are born with searing and trivial images hidden in their faces, the absence of which causes them a great deal of discomfort. It is a pain that only the brush of a face painter can alleviate, each stroke revealing the cryptic pictures in our children's faces. Any good parent knows this.

Ten years ago, the massacre came in the form of twenty-five silverback gorillas set loose at the height of the picnic. Among the fatalities was a young girl by the name of Louise Morris, who was torn to pieces. Perhaps it was Louise's performance as Mary in the Christmas pageant of the preceding winter, or perhaps it was the grim look on the faces of the three silverback gorillas that tugged her arms and legs in opposite directions, or perhaps it was just that she was so much prettier and more well behaved than the other children who were killed that day—but whatever the case, Louise Morris's death had a profound impact on the community.

That year, the town meetings grew into full-blown rallies. Louise Morris's picture ran on the front page of local newspapers every day for a month. We wore yellow ribbons to church and a local novelty shop began selling REMEMBER LOUISE T-shirts, which were quickly fashionable. Under extreme pressure from the city council, the local zoo was forced to rid itself of its prized gorilla family, Gigi, Taffy, and their newborn baby Jo-Jo, who were sold to the St. Louis Zoo, Calgary Zoo, and Cleveland Zoo, respectively.

The school board added a three-day weekend to the district calendar in memoriam of Louise and successfully carried out a protest campaign against a school two districts away, demanding that they change their mascot from the Brightonville Gorillas to the Brightonville Lightning Bolts. Without any formal action from the school board, the opposition to teaching evolution in public schools began to enjoy a sudden, regional popularity. Without any written mandate, with only the collective moral outcry of the community to guide them, teachers slowly began removing from their classrooms the laminated posters that pictured our supposed, all-too-gorilla-like ancestors as they lumbered their way across the prehistoric landscape.

The community's reaction to Louise's death was so strong that, in time, it was hard to keep track of all the changes it had engendered. It was difficult to know where one change ended and another began. Perhaps it was our hatred of gorillas that eventually gave way to our distrust of large men with bad posture, which led to the impeachment of Mayor Castlebach. Perhaps our general fear of distant countries, the forests of which were either known or suspected to support gorilla populations, had more to do with the deportation of those four Kenyan exchange students than any of us cared to admit. With all the changes connected to Louise's death, there were many ins and outs, many complexities and half-attitudes, which made it difficult to calculate. In fact, the only thing that seemed at all the same was the Frost Mountain Picnic.

When the public meetings die down, we begin to see advertisements for next year's picnic. Naturally, the initial reaction is always more outrage. But after the advertisements persist for months and months, after we see them on billboards and on the sides of buses, after we hear the radio jingles and watch the fluff pieces about the impending picnic on the local news, our attitudes invariably begin to soften. Though no one ever comes out and says it, the collective assumption seems to be that if the picnic can be advertised with so little reservation, then the problems surrounding it must have been solved. If such a pleasant jingle can be written for it, if the news anchor can discuss it with the meteorologist so vapidly, the picnic must be harmless. Our oaths against the impending picnic become difficult to maintain. Through the sheer optimism of those advertisements, the unfortunate events of the previous year are exorcized.

Those few citizens holding on to their anger are inevitably viewed as people who refuse to move on, people who thrive on discord. When they canvass neighborhoods and approach others on the streets with brochures containing facts about previous massacres, they are called conspiracy theorists and cranks. They're accused of remembering events creatively, of cherry-picking facts in order to accommodate their paranoid fantasies. Or else, it might be said of them that they have some valid points, which would bear consideration, if only their methods weren't so obnoxious, if only they didn't insist on holding up signs at street corners and putting fliers under our windshield wipers, if only they didn't look so self-righteous and affirmed in their opinions. Ultimately, the only thing that these dissenters manage to convince us of is that not to attend the picnic is to exist outside of what is normal.

* * *

In line for the boats, we wear our Remember Louise T-shirts. We busily anticipate the free corn dogs, the free ice cream cones, and the free party hats. Our children bark and grab at the passing legs of the deckhands as they move through the line in their crisp uniforms. Pale-blue pants neatly pressed, matching ties tucked into short-sleeve button-downs, the men acknowledge our children with exaggerated smiles. A deckhand drops to one knee and places his flat, white cap on a child's head. When the child screams, takes off the cap, and tries to tear it in half, the deckhand begins to laugh, as if the child has just done something delightful.

The charm of the deckhands is forced and made all the more unbelievable by our children's outrageous behavior. Desperate to have their faces painted, our children writhe on the ground and moan after the deckhands as they make their way to the loading platform. Once they reach their place beneath the awning, the deckhands occasionally look back at the long line and flash those same exaggerated smiles. They wave excitedly, a gesture that sends our children into a revitalized frenzy.

On various occasions, it has been suggested that perhaps the trouble with our children's faces is not actually a physical discomfort but an emotional discomfort similar to that of any child whose whims might be occasionally frustrated. It has been suggested that perhaps, as a rule, it may be better to do without face painting or, for that matter, anything that would cause them to act so wildly in its absence. It has been suggested that perhaps it would give our children more character if we were to let them suffer under the burden of the hidden images in their faces, forcing them to bring those images out gradually through the development of personal interests and pleasant dispositions, rather than having them only crudely painted on.

Though in the end, it's difficult for any of us to see it that way. After all, when the children wear their painted faces to school the next day, already smudged and fading, none of us wants our children to be the ones whose faces are bare. None of us wants our children to be the ones excluded or ridiculed. As good parents, we want our children to be successful, even if only in the most superficial way, as such small successes, we hope, might eventually lead to deeper, more meaningful ones. None of us wants our children to be accused of something arbitrary and most likely untrue due to the lack of some item of social significance. None of us has the confidence in our children to endure that type of thing.

None of us wants our children to become outcasts. None of us wants our children to become criminals or perverts. None of us wants our children to begin smoking marijuana or masturbating excessively. None of us wants our children to become homeless or adopt strange fetishes, driving away perfectly good mates who simply don't want to be peed on or tied down or have cigarettes put out on their backsides. None of us wants our children to begin hanging around public parks in order to steal people's dogs for some grim, unimaginable purpose. None of us wants our children to wait around outside churches after morning mass in black trench coats in order to flash the departing congregation their bruised, oversexed genitals, genitals which were once tiny and adorable to us, genitals which we had once tucked lovingly into cloth diapers. None of us wants our children dispersing crowds of elderly churchgoers with their newly wretched privates, sending those churchgoers screaming, groaning in disgust, fumbling with the keys to their Cadillacs, shielding their eyes in vain.

It isn't a judgment against people who have produced such children. It just isn't something we would want for our own. Even the parents who are less involved in their children's well-being are sick of paying the hospital bills when their unpainted children are pushed off the jungle gym or have their heads shoved into their jacket cubbies. Even those parents are sick of their kids getting nicknames like paintless, bare-face, and faggy-faggy-no-paint. Even those parents, for the most part, seem to understand.

Though the organizations and public offices in charge of the picnic remain vague and mysterious to us, it should be said that we are never directly denied information. It's simply a matter of our not knowing the right questions to ask or where to ask them.

One year, after twenty young couples were electrocuted to death in the Tunnel of Love, many of us showed up to public and private offices and demanded explanations. But in each instance, we were simply informed by a disinterested clerk that the office in question had nothing to do with the picnic and so could offer no information. Or else we were told that it had played such a small part that the only document on hand was a form reserving the park site for that particular date or a carbon copy of the event's temporary liquor license or some other trivial article.

When one of us asked where we could obtain more information or which office bore the most responsibility, the clerks offered us only a helpless look, as if to suggest that we were being unreasonable. And, truly, once we began to realize the gigantic apparatus of which each office was apparently only an incredibly small part, we had to admit that we were being unreasonable. It became clear that we were not dealing with an errant official or an ineffective ordinance, but an intersection between local government and private interests so complex that it was as if it was none of our business.

At the very most, a clerk referenced some huge, multi-national corporation said to be the primary orchestrator of the picnic. But what could be done with such information? Like that other apparatus, only on a much larger scale, such entities were too big to be properly held accountable for anything. The power of the people in charge of them was so far-reaching that by the time any one of their decisions had run its course, it was like trying to blame them for the weather. Also, because we already sensed ourselves to be a nuisance, we were reminded—a clerk pinching the bridge of his nose, and then replacing his glasses—that the walls of communication were built high around such people, and for good reason.

We wandered out of those offices in silence, our anger abated by our own embarrassment. Suddenly, we were afraid that the clerks had mistaken us for more conspiracy theorists and cranks. Mortified, many of us returned to those offices in order to apologize.

Truth be told, as compelled as each of us is to attend the Frost Mountain Picnic, for our own sake as much as for our children's, few of us ever really end up enjoying the aspects of the picnic which originally drew us there.

The craft tables, the petting zoos, the scores of musicians and wandering performers in their festively colored jerkins. Once obtained, all the much-anticipated amusements tend to seem a little trite. Even a thing as difficult to disapprove of as free food doesn't usually satisfy any of us as much as we might pretend. The fried ice creams and elephant ears are all inevitably set aside by those of us who find ourselves feeling suddenly queasy, those of us who, while waiting in line for the boats, had only recently bragged of our hunger.

On the old, wilting merry-go-round, large groups of us sit with our tongues in our cheeks and almost before the ride starts, we wish for it to be over. Even the ironic enjoyment of a child's ride seems belabored and fake. On the merry-go-round, we look to our fellow horsemen and strain forward, feigning attempts to pull ahead. Leaning dramatically from our horses, we clap hands, cheer and force out laughter so awkward and shapeless that it makes our throats ache, so high-toned and weak that it makes our eyes water.

We understand that the amusements of the Frost Mountain Picnic are supposed to entertain us. We understand that when we talk about the picnic's amusements with others, we pretend as if they do. Around water coolers and in restaurants, we repeat stories about unfinished tins of caramel corn and slow, creaking rides on the witch's wheel as if they are deeply cherished memories.

In anticipation of the free such-and-such, and the free such-and-such, we manage to convince ourselves that we are indeed looking forward to the picnic. In our minds, we falsely attach value to the items that will be given so generously. Or else, we attempt to see our participation as paying homage to something long past and romantic, a matter of heritage.

Among the difficulties we face in attempting to extricate ourselves from the Frost Mountain Picnic, a problem which is never fully addressed at the town meetings, is the fact that—just as all those offices throughout the city perform simple tasks for the picnic, but then can claim no real knowledge or responsibility—most of us are involved with the picnic on many different levels, some of which might not even be completely known to us.

Any number of local businesses, social clubs, volunteer groups, local radio stations, television stations, and departments of municipal utility are either sponsored or under-written or provided endowments by those in charge of the Frost Mountain Picnic. If we were to buy a bag of oranges from a local grocer, if we were to drop a quarter into the milk jug of the young boy standing by the automatic doors in his soccer uniform, if we were to listen to the Top 40 radio droning from the store's speakers, if we were to flip on a light switch in our own home or flush a toilet, we would be contributing in one fashion or another to the Frost Mountain Picnic. Our role is not limited to our attendance, but extends to include our inclination to drink tap water, eat fresh fruit, and go to the bathroom.

Moreover, even if we could deny ourselves these things, everywhere there are peculiar inconsistencies and non sequi-turs, which, taken together, are ominous. Periodic bank errors are reported on our checking statements next to the letters FMP and, every week, strange, superfluous deductions are made from our paychecks by an unknown entity.

A rotary club, attempting to raise money for childhood leukemia, will later check their records only to find that a majority of the proceeds was somehow accidentally sent to a cotton candy distributor in New Jersey. When the Highway Patrol calls two weeks before the picnic to ask us if we'd care to donate to the Officers' Widows Fund, the call, routed through Philadelphia, Mexico City, and Anchorage, appears on our phone bills as a seventeen-dollar charge.

We might volunteer to take part in a committee to discuss the repair of potholes throughout the city only to wind up somehow duped into preparing large mailings in the basements of public buildings, mailings which have nothing to do with potholes, but which include brochures in foreign languages with pictures of families laughing, eating corn dogs, and playing carnival games next to large, boldly colored words like *lustig* and *glücklich*.

Several times a year, men in dark blue suits flood the city. Without notice, without any noticeable regularity in their visits, they turn up everywhere. They drive slowly across town in large motorcades of black sedans with tinted windows. Dozens of them stand in line at the post office, mailing identical packages wrapped neatly in brown paper and fixed with small blue address labels. They stand outside office buildings and talk into the sleeves of their suit coats. Large groups of them sit in restaurants amid clouds of hushed laughter and cigarette smoke. The men are mostly older, but well groomed and tan, with magnificently white teeth and expensive watches. They sit three to a bench in public parks and are seen hunched over surveyors' levels outside churches and hospitals and elementary schools. The men walk in and out of every imaginable type of building at every imaginable hour for days. Then, with even less warning than their arrival, they disappear.

One hardly knows what to do with such subtleties, such phenomena. One hardly knows how to combine them or how to separate them or how to consider them in relation to one another. But whatever their sum or difference, such occurrences tend to intensify the sensation that the Frost Mountain Picnic is, in fact, unavoidable. Though it's never expressly stated, the general consensus seems to be that there's nothing we can do which would ever come to any final good, which would ever change the picnic or the massacre or whatever machinations lie beneath either.

While we ourselves feel powerless to avoid it, many of us often hope that our children might eventually outgrow the picnic. After the town meetings, most of us are already well aware that we will betray our own pledges and loyalty oaths. We leave the meetings, feeling sheepish and impotent. Though some of us do take the opportunity to stop and talk quietly with one another about the possibility that the next generation might eventually rise up and break the pattern of our complacency.

On the way home from the picnic, with the ring of mortar fire still in our ears or the stink of gorillas or gunpowder in our noses, we steal glances at our sleeping children in the backseats of our station wagons and minivans. Typically, we are bandaged from some close brush with the massacre, our arms in slings improvised out of our torn and battered REMEMBER LOUISE T-shirts. Our lips split, our noses bloodied, our palms sweaty on the steering wheel. We recall the first moments of the massacre, the first explosion, the first gunshot, the first creeping hum of the planes, the earth moving beneath our feet. We watch our children sleeping in the rearview, moonlight passing over their peaceful faces. Through the unsightly globs of paint, we catch a glimpse of how our children seemed before the picnic endowed them with such an eager, selfish spirit.

When it comes time to leave the highway, as we drift slowly toward our exit, we are tempted to jerk the wheel in the other direction and speed off to some distant city, a place untouched by picnics. We know our husbands and wives wouldn't say a word, wouldn't ask for an explanation, wouldn't even turn their heads to watch our exit as it passes, but would keep their eyes forward, like ours, a look of exhilaration on their faces.

However, these fantasies are as appealing as they are unlikely, and so our hope remains tied in to our children. Our children, who took their first steps while waiting in line for the boats, who muttered their first words to the face painters and jugglers, who lost their first teeth in the picnic's saltwater taffy and red-rope licorice. Our children, who, as they grow older, begin to explain the picnic to us as if we don't understand it. Our children, who have begun to scorn and mock us if we so much as mention Frost Mountain, snap their gum and laugh with their friends, as if our old age and presumed irrelevance threaten the very existence of the picnic.

A horn sounds, signaling the line to move forward. No matter how long we wait for the boats, or how eager we might seem, there is always a slight pause between the sounding of the horn and the eventual lurching forward of the crowd. It is a moment in which we recall the year some of the boats capsized as they left the picnic, how everyone aboard trusted the surprisingly bulky life jackets and sank to the bottom of the river like stones. It is a moment of looking from side to side, a moment of coughing and shrugging.

On the opposite shore, a small orchestra of men in dark suits begins to play the second movement of Beethoven's *Eroica*. Assembled under a large carnival tent, the men play expertly. Those whose parts have not yet come stand perfectly still or adjust the dark glasses on the bridge of their nose or speak slowly into the sleeves of their suit coat. The music sounds strange over the noise of the river. It weighs heavily in the air.

It is a moment of clarity and anxiety, in which we hope that something will deliver us from our sense of obligation toward the picnic, the sense of embarrassment that would proceed from removing our children from the line, evoking tantrums so fierce as to be completely unimaginable. It is a moment in which we wait for some old emotion to well up in us, some passion our forefathers possessed that made them unafraid of change, no matter how radical or how dangerous or—the deckhands gesturing for us to move forward, their faces suddenly angry and impatient—how impossible.

LIFE IN THE HAREM

· · · · · · · · · · ·

To begin with, I am a man. However, to say that my presence in the harem is odd simply because the king is devotedly heterosexual would hardly convey how completely inexplicable is my appointment. I hold no illusions about myself. There is nothing in my appearance that one would expect to elicit desire. Formerly one of the king's clerks, I have spent most of my life huddled over a ledger, and so my back has developed a hunch. My hands are calloused from smoothing parchment with pumice, scarred from my habit of sharpening quills with a knifepoint too hastily. I have a pronounced paunch. My skin and the whites of my eyes have yellowed. My teeth are crooked and, as if just for good measure, the Almighty saw fit to make me bald, except for a faint spray of hair over the back of my neck and behind my ears, an area of my scalp prone, for whatever reason, to dry skin and painful outbreaks of pimples. So why me?

That much was never explained to me. One night, I was simply dragged from my bed by two of the king's guards. I tried to imagine what crime I could have committed, but the only thing that came to mind as the guards pulled me through the darkened corridors of the palace, our progress lit by the glow of their lamps, was a beautiful spring afternoon two months prior, which I had spent staring stupidly out a window.

On that day, the king had been down among the offices of the clerks, discussing with my superiors the possibility of constructing a massive bridge over a broad river—a convenience that would have allowed him quicker access to the woods to the north of the palace. An avid hunter, the king was insistent on the matter even after my superiors had explained to him the different ways in which such a project would have been a financial impossibility. The debate over the bridge was an intense one, though my superiors were forced to proceed with the humility that their duty often demands of them, beginning each point and counterpoint by saying, "Of course Your Highness is wise enough to realize" and "It could not possibly have escaped your majesty's shrewdness . . ."

The difficult task of managing all the practical aspects of his kingdom has long been delegated to the king's advisors, men like my superiors. And so, all that is left for the king to manage is his own pleasure. No doubt, for a man so in touch with his own desires, conversations such as these are taxing. During his arguments for the bridge, the king shouted violently, sometimes stopping to upend a chair or knock one of my superiors to the floor. The king is a giant, bear-like man: powerful arms and legs, stomach exuberantly fat. Outbursts of this sort are as common as they are frightening—but on that day in particular, I found it difficult to pay attention to the spectacle of the king's tantrum.

Like the other clerks, I was expected to remain quietly at my station—a small desk cluttered with papers to be tended to, royal memoranda to be copied—while the king raged at the other end of the room. I was seated next to a window overlooking one of the palace's many gardens. Outside, the trees were swaying in a light, broken rhythm with the breeze. A bird swooped down, describing a soft, curved line in the air. Through that window there seemed to be something deeply suggestive about the world, and I could feel my face grow hot. I was lulled into a sort of dreaminess, when suddenly a noise escaped my throat. A moan.

I have no memory of the sound itself, but it must have been loud enough to interrupt the king's waves of abuse. All eyes were on me at once. My superiors glared at me with their lips pressed together tightly, as if to communicate that—if they survived their most recent audience with the king—their sole object would be to punish me for this especially misplaced impudence. But the king only regarded me in an inexpressive silence. He was still holding a chair over his head, which he had been brandishing at one of my superiors. But the more the king watched me, the less he looked intent on bashing them to death. He set the chair down and continued to look at me, and I did not lower my eyes. In my fear, I could neither move nor rid my face of its lurid expression. The king seemed as if he wished to address me in some way, as if he wished to address the sound that I had just made. Then he looked suddenly embarrassed and left the room. In the weeks that followed, the king lost all interest in the prospect of a bridge and never spoke of it again.

So on the night of my abduction, this incident of the moan was the only one in which I could imagine myself having actually transgressed against the king. But how does one confess to a crime if the king already knows the extent of it? More than that, how does one confess to a crime that he himself does not fully understand?

But the guards were not interested in receiving any such confession. Instead, they forced me to undress. They jeered at my naked body and wondered aloud what had gotten into the king. They then handed me a small bundle, which was to be my costume in the harem: a thin, billowy pair of pants, a tasseled fez, and a half vest that enhanced the low slope of my belly as well as the painful, buzzard-like angle of my neck.

The guards pushed me through a narrow door into a large, moonlit room. They sealed the door behind me, and without their lamps I could see nothing in the silvery blue darkness of the women's quarters. But as my eyes adjusted to the faint light of the moon, I saw rising out of that darkness hundreds and hundreds of canopied beds, couches, tents like small cities in the distance, and—on them, in them, alongside them—countless women, fast asleep.

* * *

Every evening, in the harem, a bell is rung and the women and I are gathered into a long double column that stretches in a great line across the quarters. Certainly, there is the typical fare: young, nubile women with full breasts beneath jeweled halters and exquisitely round, pear-like stomachs.

However, in addition to these standard, if not somewhat clichéd, beauties, the king has added women, girls really, young enough to cause a scandal. He has added women old enough to be his mother, women old enough to be his grandmother. He has added excruciatingly thin, bird-like women, and women as large as mountains.

In the harem, there are many women missing odd numbers of body parts, whom the king will often call up to his chamber two or three at a time in inexhaustible combinations. Tonight: woman with no arms and woman with no ears. Tomorrow, perhaps: one leg and no legs, or seven toes and half a tongue, or one eye, no teeth, and hole in throat. To these permutations he will also rotate in the women in his possession having been born with extra body parts, which creates a dizzying number of possibilities, especially when one considers that within these variables—no eyes, extra arm, no mouth, two noses—there are also the variables mentioned above: no eyes is extremely thin, extra arm perhaps too young, no mouth somehow fat, two noses almost elderly.

At first, I assumed all this to mean that the king might have a flare for the grotesque, which would then explain my own presence in the harem. But no matter how unusual many of these women may be, they are all undeniably beautiful. A woman with no arms combs her long, auburn hair with a silver comb gripped in her left foot. A woman with no fingers rests her head in her right palm. Leaning on the marble ledge of a balcony, she hums absently to herself and begins to smile. When it comes to the beauty of women, one must understand that the poets were wrong. The comeliness of women is described in the great poems as a balance of perfect features, a harmony of ideal movements. However, the women of the harem cause one to understand that the beauty of women relies on no such balance, no such harmony. Rather, it is an elusive essence that can expand and contract to fill any vessel.

I should admit, though, I am no expert on the subject of women. Before I was appropriated to the harem, I had only seen one woman in the nude. While riding through the provinces on one of the many errands required of my position then, I passed through a small village where I happened to see, through the window of a cottage with one heavy shutter inadvertently thrown open, an older, bare-chested woman stooping to pick up a child. The sight of that woman, moving with such ease and frankness, had been tantalizing. Many nights afterward, I would remain awake in my bed, tortured by the image of that woman as well as by my sense of guilt at having witnessed her in the midst of such a savage privacy. It was not unlike my experience here in the harem, and the sense of both wonder and dread that falls over me as I observe these astonishing women.

The point is: The king is obviously a great admirer of beauty in all its unlimited forms and it is on account of this admiration—and not some tendency toward the grotesque—that he surrounds himself with such women. That is why, even if the king was to take on a man as a lover, it makes no sense that it would be me, such a wretched and consummately unbeautiful creature. If he so wished, he could surround himself with whole armies of beautiful young men.

Once the women and I are assembled, a group of three guards then examines the column with orders as to which of us is to be taken up to the king's chamber. In my first few weeks in the harem, I was never chosen, though the two lower-ranking guards would often stop and mock me while the third and chief guard—the one principally responsible for carrying out the king's selections, consulting a series of charts and papers when choosing the women from the column—would only deliver me an occasional unhappy look. Without words, his eyes seemed to explain as he moved full of purpose down the column: not you. Not yet.

In those early days, my time in the harem was spent in the grips of two different anxieties. The first was that I was surrounded by beautiful women, who all filled me with desire. Of course, I did not intend to impose myself on these women, nor were they cynical enough to assume that I would. If anything, the women of the harem accepted me into their quarters graciously. Their kindness exacerbated this anxiety. The fact that these women wanted only to live politely alongside me—a generous impulse on their part—produced in me an immense shame on account of my lust for them. Shame, because I could not prevent myself from following them with my eyes, from being captivated by their every movement through the quarters, from being charmed by the sound of their voices in conversation, from being set aflame by the smell of petals and camphor as they passed. A woman stood near a small fountain bathing her chest while talking to a companion. I watched as the water ran down her pleasantly small breasts. The bather's companion, having noticed me, whispered something into her ear. The bather then discreetly turned her back to me and continued to wash. It was not with disgust or outrage that the women of the harem reacted to my desire, but with this quiet practicality. They tended to cover themselves in my presence and act modestly. They tried to protect me from their nudity out of a mature restraint, as if they were trying to avoid being cruel to an animal.

And if my first anxiety was that I was full of desire, then my second anxiety was that—somewhere in the palace, in some mysterious fashion—I was desired. Was I to be one of the king's lovers? Before I knew the touch of a woman or the sound of a kind word from her mouth, was I to know the touch of this man?

At these thoughts, I realized what it was to be the object of an unwanted desire. My desire for the women of the harem was as unwanted by them as the king's was by me. This, of course, lent to my lust another degree of shame. Because I was too weak to look away when a young woman absently scratched her thigh, unintentionally raising her hem, because I could not make my intentions less obvious when I dawdled by the various fountains and baths, I was tormenting these women with the same disquiet and self-consciousness that tormented me on account of the king.

At times, I wished that I was immune to this desire, that I was a eunuch. Then, the sight of the women in the quarters would not tempt me at all. Their images would reach my mind, but they would signify nothing. I would be happily set apart from them, and thus be able to return the cool looks of nonrecognition that I received from them so frequently. Watching their hips revolve across the marble floor of the quarters would be as plain and uninteresting to me as observing the cogs of a mill. Smelling the collective fragrance of their bodies would be little more enticing to me than the mild stink of mushrooms at the base of a tree. Perhaps there would be something almost sickening about their womanliness, like the scurry of insects back into the earth when a rock is overturned. But then a woman across the quarters would let down her hair and I would fight the urge to cradle the locus of my desire in my hands, to protect it.

I was in the harem for almost two months before I was called up to the king's chamber. One night, when the women and I were gathered into our column, I was again singled out by two of the king's guards. At first, I only anticipated their usual rounds of abuse. But when I saw the king's principal guard look over his charts and back at me—delivering the two lesser guards a brisk nod—I immediately began to despair.

As I was led into the outer corridor, my mind was occupied with that mix of fear and shame in which I saw the king's desire for me as analogous to my desire for the women of the harem. I thought again of the woman in the cottage stooping to pick up her child, my intrusion into that private scene: a woman, bare-chested, freckled skin, faint down of hair along her arms ablaze in sunlight. I remembered the flash of exhilaration that I had felt after seeing her. This memory gave way, again, to shame. I pictured the king sitting on my horse outside that cottage, while inside I was the one stooping bare-chested to pick up a child. Lifting the child, I recognized the desire I had inadvertently produced in the king, which was actually my own desire, and felt cold. As I walked down the halls of the palace with the guards on either side of me, moving on my own two feet toward some degradation that I could scarcely imagine, I saw myself as the child being lifted. I saw the fear in my mother's eyes and knew that, though I was being lifted, I was also on a horse outside, leering as I passed. I grew dizzy, imagining the scene again and again until I found myself—an abrupt stop, the guards calling for me to halt—standing before the king's chamber door.

Inside, the king sat at a writing desk. His shoulders were slumped beneath a heavy robe and he leaned intently over a scattering of papers. He did not turn to acknowledge my arrival or the guards' departure but continued to examine the documents at his desk. The light in the room came from a brass candelabrum, which the king occasionally moved in order to accommodate his reading, an act which bent and shifted the shadows about the room, slowly revealing to me the king's chamber, filled with its countless hunting trophies. Rising and falling in the wavering dark were antlers, boar tusks, elaborate arrangements of teeth and claws on plaques of polished oak. In that uncertain light, the massive bed in the center of the room seemed to tremble and breathe as its fox-fur blankets gave off the captured musk of all the king's previous exertions.

In a low, quiet voice, the king ordered me to remove my clothes.

My costume lent itself to hasty removal. Even with my slight reluctance, I took it off in one brisk movement. In an effort to preserve my dignity, I covered my genitals with my hands. But I had forgotten to remove my fez, and so I stood there—a plucked turkey of a man—looking even more ridiculous than I could have supposed.

Naked and in the dark, I thought about the women of the harem. Did this sort of thing not affect them or, like me, did the circumstance of standing without one's clothes in the presence of the king make them feel as if their bodies were not their own? Standing in the king's chamber, did those parts of their bodies that had once seemed so natural to them suddenly seem cumbersome? My genitals hung clumsily beneath my palms and felt impossibly foreign. Did their breasts and hips, which had once seemed so innately a part of themselves—part of the simplicity and joy of their own skin—suddenly seem an imposition, another joke played on them by the desirous one?

The king gestured toward a pile of clothes folded neatly on the floor, indicating that I was to put them on. To my surprise, they seemed to be items from the king's own wardrobe. I recognized immediately the heavy robe with its velvet trim, the cherry-red pantaloons, the loose silk shirt and elaborately embroidered doublet. They were, in point of fact, an exact copy of the clothes that the king was wearing at that moment, though having been altered to fit someone much smaller. I knew nothing of what the king had in store for me, but even in my most optimistic suppositions, I had assumed that he would be making use of me in the nude. Once I was dressed, having traded my fez for a crown, the king rose and commanded me to take his place at the writing desk.

Seated, I was able to see more clearly the papers the king had been examining. They comprised a roster of the harem's inhabitants. There were some that seemed rather complicated, in which descriptions of women were arranged in circles and overlapping triangles or by season and the phases of the moon. But among these smaller, ancillary documents was one massive chart divided into three columns. In the first was a succession of dates. In the second, a grouping of women: no legs and extremely thin, three arms and no teeth, no fingers and extra tongue. In the third was a varying number of intricately drawn **penises** corresponding to each date and grouping of women. **On the** night of extremely young with hole in throat and extremely old with extra leg, the king had drawn seven penises. The scale itself ranged from one penis to roughly thirty.

Just as I began to observe this chart more closely, the king asked me to pick it up. I did so reluctantly. With the chart in my hand he ordered me to moan.

That was it. I moaned for a little over an hour and he watched in silence. The king was so transfixed by my moan that the force of his presence and authority seemed to shrink from the room, until it was as if he existed only in that sound rising up from my throat. Afterward, he seemed weak. His voice was a dry whisper. He ordered me to change back into my costume, whereupon I was returned to my place in the women's quarters.

My first assumption was that the king, having joined himself with so many beautiful women, had rendered himself dead to pleasure, the way a wealthy man might feel bored with money or even burdened by it. I thought the king might see his exertions with the women of the harem as the source not of pleasure but of an aching back and sore member. This would explain why the king had called upon me, a person whose desire is still intact.

But I soon abandoned this first assumption. A man who joins himself with two to three women every night and yet still manages to lean over a ledger and draw genitalia into the late hours of the night is clearly not a man whose desire has failed him. Rather, such behavior suggests that the king is being driven mad with desire. Perhaps he is running methodically through all those combinations of women not out of a festive sense of variety but in an attempt to solve his desire like a riddle.

The king rates his encounters not only with drawings of whole penises but fractions of penises. The nature of the king's frustration may be that he recognizes the difference between a night worth ten penises and one worth ten and a half. Once distinctions such as that open up, they never stop. Suddenly everything defies categorization. I saw one entry in particular that bore several whole penises and then one almost inscrutable tip.

It would make sense that the king would experience a type of catharsis by watching his frustration move into a proxy—namely, me—thus freeing himself from it temporarily. After all, consider the content of my moan. Even before I was forced to live in the harem, I possessed an eager and impossible desire, a yearning for release that I barely understood beyond the nightly, untaught fumbling of my fingers against my own member in the dark. It was this desire, finally, that caused me to moan by that window on that lovely spring day and that the king naturally recognized as comparable to his own desire. So the king, exhausted, has decided to grant himself a respite through the performance of my moan. Such an action appears to grant him a release beyond release, as release itself has become an indecipherable burden.

After having been called up to the king's chamber for the first time, I thought that living alongside the women of the harem might be somewhat less difficult. I still found myself troubled by my lust for them, but—because I had been used by the king—I felt a certain camaraderie, which caused them to seem more approachable, more open to my frail attempts at civility. I saw them as more than forms to be desired. I recognized their full womanhood, in which they became everything at once: mothers, daughters, sisters, wives. It was in this expansive mood that I approached one woman, sitting on the lip of a fountain. She was excruciatingly thin with her long, dark hair gathered over one shoulder, toes dangling in the water.

Hoping to commiserate, I asked if it bothered her to be kept in the women's quarters against her will. She laughed—the way one laughs at a child who has said something ridiculous.

"Where else would the king keep me?" she said.

"No," I said, "does it bother you to be kept here for the king's pleasure? Does it bother you to be treated like this?"

The woman, who had been looking at me until then with patience in her eyes, looked down into the water abruptly as if she were suddenly annoyed.

"Women are treated like this everywhere. Here, we share the burden of one man. Out there, every man is our burden."

"Out there, you are not slaves."

"Worse," she said. "We are wives, sisters, daughters, mothers. Out there, every expectation of every man is another lash of the whip."

I was struck by the coldness in the woman's voice, the certainty with which she described such a hopeless vision of the world. Without saying a word, I withdrew from her. She continued to stare down at the surface of the water, made turbulent by the relentless jet of the fountain.

It wounded me to know that even by attempting to replace my lust with a more tender appreciation for the women of the harem, I was apparently still binding them to something repellent. I was still very much like the king, who—although he did not use me in a strictly sexual sense—kept me bound to a bizarre ritual for his own benefit. Were the expectations of men toward women—wife, sister, mother, daughter—just more bizarre rituals? As much as I sympathized with the woman by the fountain, I could not believe that to be true. I could not divorce myself from the hope that the world could be made more pleasant by a gentle living side by side. Wife. Sister. Mother. Daughter. In my mind, I had not regarded these titles as prison sentences but as communions. Husband. Brother. Father. Son. And yet, neither could I fully dismiss her notion of the world, neither could I bring myself to say that it was foolishness.

I continued to return to the king's chamber several nights a week. Our interactions remained unexplained by him. Each night was a play to be interpreted later, after I had left the stage.

On several occasions the king incorporated acts which suggested that he was, in fact, simply losing his mind. One night, he made me eat a handful of feathers. Another night, we spent four hours rearranging the furniture in his chamber. Yet another night, he had me hit him in the mouth with a board.

It stood to reason that the king was deliberately trying to convince me that he was insane. Because his inability to conquer his own desire would cause him to seem weak, it was in his interest to prevent me from understanding my true purpose in his chamber. Though it also occurred to me that perhaps the king was actually losing his mind, that his desire was driving him mad.

But no matter how strange our interactions became, the majority of our time together was still organized around my moan, my looking at his chart. Perhaps, through the release that my performances provided him, the king was attempting to make a final stand against both his madness and his desire.

My anxiety over these performances diminished for the most part, and I immediately recognized this indifference as a terrible loss on my part. Along with it, my shame began to diminish. Back in the harem, I stared at the women openly. That fleeting sense of kinship disappeared, and I suddenly felt that the woman by the fountain was right. I sat unabashedly with my feet in that same fountain, watching the women bathe with my mouth agape. At night, I conjured up the day's collected images—the bodies of the harem women—and pulled angrily at myself.

In the months before I was appropriated to the harem, it was not uncommon for me to lie in my bed at night and think about that woman from the cottage. Through my guilt, I would whisper sweet things to her in the emptiness of my bed. I would dream her there and then say those sweet things as if she wanted to hear them. As if, by saying them, I was doing a great kindness to her. Now, when pulling at myself in some dark corner of the quarters, I think of women without faces. I bare my teeth. I curse and make empty threats at no one. While I have always held my own worth in doubt, I cannot help but feel that some goodness that was in me is slipping away. An innocence that I simultaneously long for and dismiss.

* * *

Earlier this week, the king took up a new practice. As if to add to my confusion, the king disguised himself as me. When I changed into his clothes, he changed into mine. I was required to command him to moan at the chart. When he followed the commands I was required to give, I was then required to watch him with interest, to mime a sensation of tremendous release. This development no doubt made sense to the king, who wished me to assume the full burden of his desire.

Tonight, as I stood dressed in the king's clothing, a guard escorted a young woman into the room. The guard led the girl to the bed and then turned to me, bowing in mock deference. The king, dressed as me, bowed as well. Then the guard led him away, presumably back to the harem.

When I enter the king's chamber, I know I am entering the fever dream of his desire. If upon entering he were to ask me to recite a poem that had been written on the walls in excrement, I would do it without surprise. But standing over that beautiful woman, who wore a half vest that I recognized immediately as like my own, her bare stomach rising and falling, I was amazed. It was one thing for the king to share his clothing with me, his charts—but it was quite another for him to ask me to join myself to one of the women of the harem.

I lay next to the young woman on the bed and felt only a trace of my former shame. In addition to a vest she wore those same billowy pants, the same tasseled fez. Seeing her dressed in this way reminded me of the empathy I had felt toward the women of the harem, the unease I had felt at being—as I had then believed myself to be—an object of the king's desire.

Whatever the case, I ignored my scant sense of shame. After all, I had been ordered to impose myself on the woman, had I not? Refusing to go through with the performance would only put the woman in danger by angering the king, would it not? These were the questions I distracted myself with while my mind gave itself over to the notion of enjoying a woman's body.

The chance lines of her thighs beneath the loose fabric. The perfect bell of her hips as I unfastened her at the waist and pulled her free. The vest almost springing open on its own. In my mind, there was a growing ferocity toward the woman, which caused me to believe that my former sense of shame in the harem had not been on account of the fact that my desire for these women had been wrong, but that it had been unrequited. In that moment, I felt I understood that my shame had not been because—in my lust—I had been treating the women unfairly, but because—in my wretchedness—I had been powerless to treat them as I wished.

I joined myself to the woman. And despite all my suspicions with respect to the king and his desire, I still anticipated for myself—somehow—a final release, something whole and perfect. But just as I began to squirm and writhe on top of the woman, I knew that this encounter would be as unsatisfying as my nights spent cursing in the dark. Whose fault was this? Certainly not the woman's. Her movements beneath me were, though perfunctory and clearly stemming from a kind of patience, made superb by the grace of her body's youth. If I was displeased, I knew that displeasure to be my own doing.

The seed of this dissatisfaction grew in me. The knowledge that my release with this woman would be like my other, smaller releases—pathetic, brief, solitary no matter how much imagination I exercised—made my limbs feel heavy. I knew then that I was experiencing the first touch of whatever was driving the king to these absurd heights. Also, I knew that the woman beneath me was not too young or too old. She had no extra body parts and none were missing. With the exception of being beautiful, she was normal. From this, I understood that she was merely a point of departure, that next would be the woman with the extra this, the woman with the missing that, the limitless combinations, those obscene charts. As I struggled toward a release that did not await me, a hopeless expanse began to open beneath me. I thought of that bare-chested woman in her cottage. I was envious of that young man on his horse, before he looked through that window. I was envious of that day when I did not yet know fully what a woman looked like, when I did not yet know fully what a man was or what, through carelessness, one could become. No matter how selfishly I grabbed at the woman beneath me, no matter how frantically I forced myself into her and attempted to take root, still that infinite space was welling up and setting me adrift.

THOSE OF US IN PLAID

. . . .

Our job was simple: get the monkey in the capsule. Our superiors made sure to point out that it was one of the easiest and therefore least important tasks, a task that anyone could do, just as they always pointed out that our plaid coveralls were not as sharp-looking as their coveralls. But we felt that every step of the sequence was equally important, that, coveralls aside, everyone involved shared an integral role in the project's success. After all, if we didn't get the monkey in the capsule, then the capsule couldn't be sent to the first prep station. If the capsule never made it to the first prep station, then it'd never get to the Transport Operator, who would end up sitting there in his hydraulic lift, empty-handed, chewing on his moustache and writing swear words on his clipboard. If the capsule never made it to transport, it'd never get to the Project Elects in their snazzy red coveralls, whose job it was to slap the thermal readers on the capsule and signal the helicopter to come round and pick the damn thing up. Which would mean the pilot would just have to keep circling, wasting gas. He'd probably end up crashing before he realized he'd run out of time to fly the capsule over the volcano and drop it in. And if the capsule never made it up with the helicopter and down into the volcano, then the Advanced Project Elects, in their stunning blue coveralls with silver piping and decals in exquisite copper brown, wouldn't have any occasion to flip the detonator on the incendiary bomb planted along the throat of the volcano. The whole experiment would be ruined.

And in fact that's exactly what did happen. We never got that monkey in there.

It was embarrassing, watching all those Project Elects throw their headsets down onto the tarmac, their obscenities obscured by the sirens of all the fire engines racing toward the wrecked chopper. We knew we'd never hear the end of it.

As it was, we couldn't get through a whole day without having to suffer some kind of abuse from the Project Elects. They were always calling us the most awful names or putting us into headlocks and making us smell their farts. Ned, our group leader, had to be hospitalized after some Project Elects put hornet pheromone in our hand sanitizer. Ned likes to eat his lunch outside and had hardly unwrapped his ham and cheese before they were on him. The poor guy had to get twenty-eight stingers removed from his hands and face. None of the Project Elects apologized when the people in Human Resources told Ned that our insurance policy didn't cover insect attacks. And when he returned a week later, covered in gauze? They put Monistat in his coffee.

They made up songs about us constantly and drew penises on the pictures of our wives and children that they stole out of our lockers. Sometimes they took the apples out of our lunch boxes, dipping them in the toilet, drying them off, and replacing them without telling us. In any given year, it was impossible to say just how many toilet apples we might have eaten.

But worse than these simple degradations was that we would have given anything to be exactly like them: their back-slapping, their cocksure attitudes, their dashing good looks and idiotic jokes. We would imagine we *were* them, allowing our minds to drift for a moment toward thoughts of ourselves smoking with our feet up in the break room, discussing the finer points of the project with the other Elects. And then we would look down at our plaid coveralls and remember once again our own intractable lameness.

Still, regardless of everything experience had taught us, we hoped that one day we'd deliver the beaker filled with strange liquid to the testing facility so promptly and so without incident, or paint the numbers on the capsule so perfectly and so without dribbles, that we would somehow win them over. That we'd begin receiving invitations to their famed barbecues, or to a raucous birthday party at the nudie bar near the airport. We held on, each of us, to the distant possibility that we might perform well enough to become Project Elects ourselves, thus abandoning our hideous plaid coveralls, designed specifically to designate us as the grunts of the project. Maybe replacing them with yellow coveralls or red ones or, God help us, blue.

So it was with this total commitment and total willingness to please our betters that we took on the monkey as our charge.

As far as tasks went, it certainly wasn't the worst. Almost immediately, we liked the monkey. In addition to it being our inevitable responsibility to load him into the capsule for his descent into the volcano, it was also our job to take care of him until all other preparations were complete. And in doing so we were struck right away by how prepossessing the monkey seemed. How patient with captivity. He sat in his cage and observed us soberly, with a subtle curiosity. When we presented him with food, he received it gratefully, with a chatter that seemed almost friendly.

Before long, the monkey warmed to us completely. His cage became little more than a pretense; he moved around our workstation freely. He sat on our shoulders, searching our scalps for jiggers with a visible show of concern. We bought a lounge chair with our own money, and he would sit in our laps while we read to him out of *Reader's Digest*. Of course, he didn't understand any of it, but he seemed to like the attention. He would stay perched on our laps, his eyes fixed on us as we read, his mouth hanging open slightly. Whenever we finished reading, he would take the magazine from our hands, put it on his head, and just screech and screech. We would laugh and he would screech. Laugh. Screech. Laugh. Screech.

The only problem was that as we grew closer to the monkey, the idea of dropping him into a volcano and then blowing him up seemed, more and more, to be unbearably cruel. It seemed like a waste, destroying a perfectly good monkey—not to mention one to whom we had become so recently attached. The Project Elects assured us that dropping the monkey into the volcano was important. They scribbled impatiently on the blackboard in the demonstration room. They drew a picture of the monkey peeking out of the capsule's small window and smiling. They drew themselves standing on the tarmac and smiling. They drew a picture of us having wild sex with each other in the locker room and smiling. Look, they said, everybody's happy. And if our own happiness wasn't enough to make us put the monkey in the capsule, they reminded us that we were replaceable, that we were, in fact, desirable only in the sense that we were so totally capable of being replaced, that we were all a bunch of yo-yos, that we were lucky to know there even *was* a monkey.

It didn't help that as soon as we expressed an interest in the monkey's well-being, the Project Elects started demanding time alone with him. They would kick us out of our work-station, insisting they had tests to conduct. We would come back later to find them drinking Pabst and trying to peg the monkey with empties. One afternoon, we found them in there with a keg and the small defibrillator that had been used for the dachshund experiment four months earlier. After they left, punching shoulders and grab-assing with one another on their way out the door, the monkey seemed deeply shaken. It took thirty minutes and seven Baby Ruths just to get him out of his cage. We tried to read to him, but he only clung to our chests in the lounge chair, eventually letting out one long, exhausted breath and falling uncertainly to sleep.

But when we grew quiet and regretful, the Project Elects would catch us staring doubtfully at the monkey and clap us on the back of the head. They would tell us that there was no plausible reason to be nervous. They would remind us that our job was in no way even close to brain surgery. Put the monkey in the capsule. That was it.

We imagined barbecue sauce on our fingers in beautiful backyards. We imagined the strange camaraderie brought on by booze and naked women, a dark room filled with smoke. Put the monkey in the capsule. A no-brainer.

The day we finally received orders to proceed, we let the monkey sit in the lounge chair by himself and eat as many candy bars as he could. Meanwhile we all stood in a circle and took turns reading to him. For the occasion, we picked his favorite article out of *Reader's Digest*. It was the one written by an explorer who had gotten lost in Antarctica and suffered unthinkable hardships until falling in with a friendly group of penguins who had helped him to survive. We liked to think that he saw something of himself in the explorer, lost in a barren, inhospitable landscape with no real means of returning home. We also liked to think maybe he saw a little bit of us in the penguins that regurgitated fish into the explorer's mouth. Typically when we read it to him, he seemed to screech a little louder than usual, in a happy way, or hop up onto our shoulders and pull tenderly at our ears. On that day, though, with the capsule prepped and glittering in the corner, he seemed to ignore the story altogether. Instead, he watched our faces, perhaps attempting to discern in them the reason behind the extra candy bars, the certain heaviness in our voices as we read.

Of course, we wished there could have been some kind of alternative. But what could we do? Not put the monkey in the capsule? Not let him spend his last moments on earth terrified and alone? Not let him get liquefied and blown up? When the article was finished, we closed the magazine and placed him in the capsule without much ceremony. We did pause briefly before securing the hatch. It felt important to give him one last remorseful look, to let him know that, while we understood that this was necessary, it also brought us no joy.

It was at that point, by all accounts, that we lost the monkey.

Maybe it was the force of that remorseful look. Maybe it was our tone of voice. Maybe it was the bottle of Pabst that one of the Project Elects had put in the capsule as a joke. Whatever the case, one second he was our special little friend, calmly sitting in the fore of the capsule—the next he was biting Ned's neck. Poor Ned, he always seems to get the worst of it.

Cleared of all sentiment, we attempted to regain control of the monkey—but he was everywhere. He was around our ankles, his feral teeth tearing through the gabardine of our coveralls. He was on top of shelves, whipping down bookends. He was darting toward us, pummeling us with his date-like fists. He jumped from one place to the next with an unfathomable quickness, pulling our hair out at the roots, throwing feces, and urinating on us from across the room with an accuracy that we would all admit to later as being completely disturbing.

Eventually, he found a toolbox that someone from maintenance must have left unattended and armed himself with a Phillips head. Sensing his advantage, he grabbed two more candy bars before backing slowly out of the room.

Once he made it to the tarmac, he used the screwdriver to stab out the eye of an Advanced Project Elect who had tried to stop him.

Horrible, horrible.

When they pulled the pilot out of the wrecked chopper with a gigantic piece of tail boom in his abdomen, we were mortified. The murky room filled with naked women disappeared in its own smoke. The barbecue sauce that had haunted our fingers revealed itself for what it really was: flecks of monkey crap thrown in anger. Our hopes were dashed, most likely forever. Though, in the disciplinary meeting much later, when they showed us the security tape of the monkey outrunning several more Elects and making it all the way to the tree line, where he stopped for a moment in order to turn toward his captors and wave his screwdriver in a mad show of freedom, we had to admit that we were glad to see him go. In the meeting room, the Elects were all disheveled and ridiculous-looking: frayed piping dragging behind them as they walked, decals dangling from their chests. We didn't look any better, of course. And with the Elects already razzing us, already gearing up for a whole new level of torment, we knew that regarding the monkey's escape as something that was somehow good was a thought that was, if not our stupidest, then at least one that served to show why we were so worthy of our superiors' contempt, why we were the ones stuck in plaid. We probably always would be.

THE MISERY OF THE CONQUISTADOR

· · · · · · · · · · ·

In a dense wood, I kill a native woman. She approaches me from behind, perhaps out of curiosity, and I brain her with my helmet. Sheer reflex. Secluded from my men, I remove her simple garments, place my forehead reverently to her pudenda, and weep.

Gold forces the hand. Eliminates the lazy, unmotivated freedom of our will. Drives us into jungles. Amidst wild men. Demands swift decisions. And yet . . .

A man throws a stone at me and flees into the safety of some brush. My men encourage me to take retribution by razing a small village to the south, but I hesitate. At this sign of weakness, the look of disgust in the eyes of my men is unbearable.

Even after we put down the village, my men seem unsure. After I set fire to the last hovel—slaying each man, woman, and child who comes bursting out, awash in flames—in the faces of my men one can still only see the recognition of that moment as I stood before them, the moment in which I listened to their arguments against the village and dithered, if only for an instant.

My weeping is interrupted by the sound of footsteps. My armor suddenly feels heavy. I manage to wipe my eyes, but a handful of my men still find me kneeling over the dead woman. My face red and damp.

Do I desire gold? No. Gold is simply what my time on earth demands of me. It is the first step in a long and rapid chain of necessities. It is essential that I collect gold, so that I might repay my benefactors, who have provided me with men and ships. Pleased, my benefactors might then provide me with more men, more ships. Having been provided with a greater means, I might then be able to collect more gold, thus repaying my benefactors for this increased means. This will induce them to send an even larger number of men and ships, which will naturally be used to collect an even larger amount of gold. Once begun, this manner of amplification will continue. More ships. More men. More gold. A fierce thrust of success and proportionate compensation spiraling upward forever. That is, until I die. My death, in turn, will create a small vacuum of success to be filled as quickly as it's created, like the bottom of a foot as it leaves a bath, the water filling the space evacuated by the foot instantaneously, delivering the foot one last suck of a kiss as it breaks the surface—so will my spirit leave this earth, with gold delivering some last, fleeting gesture of its own.

In response to a report regarding a large city to the north, I prepare my men for battle. Giant stone walls. Spears leaping over the savage bulwark like fleas. Desperate warriors in their striped smocks, charging recklessly. Somehow, I march us in the wrong direction. Instead of a city, we find a small clearing. Men and women trading goods laid out on blankets. Children playing in the dirt. An elderly man approaches me and offers to trade me a strange-looking gourd for my scabbard. Behind me, my men begin to speak quietly to one another and laugh.

Of course, I would prefer a settled life. A small cottage fixed open in the Mediterranean heat, or else shut fast against the long, difficult winters outside the brown granite walls of Ávila. Perhaps a son, standing shirtless in the late summer heat, regarding the drift of some gull in the distance—or else stoking a sweet-smelling fire playfully, his proud breath freezing in the air before him, the seams of the house whistling loudly in the midst of some storm. Certainly a wife, who would pace nude in the heat or warm herself against me in the unbearable cold—a wife, certainly, who for whatever reason would not mind the fact that my left eye is missing or that my right leg has been deformed since birth. Who would not mind that I lost the lower half of an ear in a battle fought halfway across the world on the footsteps of some giant, crude city. Who would not mind that I am often stern when the situation does not call for it or when I do not understand what is expected of me. Who would understand the necessity of my striking our boy when he lets the fire burn out or stands too long at the window, obstructing the breeze. Who would not mind that I turn glib when happy or petty when depressed. Who would not mind the fact that I often give off the distinct musk of a large animal carcass left to rot in the sun, the smell of something hollow—a pinched stink. Who would not mind bearing witness to the sheer terror and humiliation that are my every waking effort to exist as myself.

A man like me is only able to make himself palatable through success. And so, the sword. Gold, the enumeration of success. This wilderness.

Even dead, the woman is beautiful. I fight the urge to touch her mouth. Her hair. I fight the urge to lie on the ground and roll her on top of me. I fight the urge to feel her weight. Her limbs, still limp, draping down over me. As I kneel above her, my men seem uncomfortable. One of them coughs, asks me what I have done. Flustered, I lie. I tell my men that I raped the woman to death and they look relieved. They laugh and congratulate me. One stoops to cut off her head. I blanch and my men roll their eyes, as if at a boy who, having caught a fish, is afraid to remove it from its hook.

When I return, I will tell my benefactors that a clot of natives watched our arrival in awe, that they called out to us from the shore, walking off into the surf and dropping to their knees. I will claim that our landing party was greeted with deference— that the natives mistook us for gods. I will tell these false stories at banquets in halls in the most sensational terms possible. Seated next to a beautiful young woman, I will take her hand in mine and describe how the chests of the women hung bare, how the men would ravage them in plain sight, taking them where they stood. Later, I will escort the young woman through a garden or along a riverbank, explaining how the natives who witnessed our landing, upon seeing a crucifix, screamed as if being burnt. I will tell her how I held giant monsters of men in my arms, how I whispered softly to them as they wept, as they begged in their outlandish tongue to be admitted into the Kingdom of Heaven. In reality, the few natives who witnessed our landing hardly took notice. Three young men stood on the beach, talking quietly to one another and squinting at the sun's glare on our armor, as if annoyed. By then, however, it will not matter. The young woman will become overwhelmed, her face hot to the touch. She will move to speak or to embrace me or to flee from me in horror—but not before I grab her roughly, pressing something into her hand. She will hold her breath as I slide the gift of a coin into her palm. Gold.

In a dense wood, I kill a woman. She approaches me from behind, perhaps out of curiosity, while I place the palm of my hand on a tree trunk, imagining a clearing and a shipyard, a fortress and a gallows. A young woman approaches me from behind, her bare feet moving soundlessly over the hard earth. I touch a tree, soon to be felled and shaped for Spain. I feel the spark of a dreadful strength within me. I am the master of a new world, bending the fates of lesser peoples. My armor clings to me as fast as my own skin, less a man than an engine of war. I am clever and yet unthinking. I am invulnerable and yet wounded with a terrible rage. I am both a force of nature and above it. A young woman approaches from behind, and I whirl round, striking her with my helmet. It happens quickly. On the ground she's still smiling, still eager to greet me.

One of my men picks up the woman's head and pitches it further into the woods. He lets out a loud grunt, and the head goes soaring in a long, easy arc. It drifts to the left and thumps against a tree, sending it into a slow spiral, fanning out its shock of lovely black hair that turns a burnt amber as it passes into the sunlight. The head continues on out of sight and eventually lands with a soft thud.

* * *

My arm around the waist of the young woman from the banquet. My hand still pressing the coin into hers. What will happen next? The noise of the river rising up around us. Some low branch dropping petals. Perhaps she struggles. To escape? To adjust herself? To achieve a position that will allow me more purchase? She turns from me abruptly as I attempt to kiss her mouth. The coin falls into the dirt. I take her face in my hand and pull her violently to my mouth, her lips soft and motionless. I lean over her, forcing myself against her. Almost falling. Finally she offers me a kiss. After which, without much prompting, her head comes off in my hands. The noise of the river still rising, the petals still dropping, I meet the startled gaze of her head with my own. Or perhaps her kiss slowly turns sour, until I am forced to turn away from her and vomit in the grass. Perhaps her teeth begin to come loose in my mouth. Perhaps her hair, once pulled, comes out in clumps. Whatever the case, the fantasy is never agreeable for very long. The only aspect of it that remains unspoiled is the image of the coin being pressed into the woman's hand. I avoid dwelling on it for fear of eventually drifting to another one of those horrible kisses, the woman's tongue turning to ash in my mouth—but on occasion I allow myself to relive the imagined sensation of that perfect coin against her palm, the weight of that relentless gold. Often, the sensation of the woman's hand fades and in my mind I begin to press the coin into nothing. I stand alone in the fantasy, forcing that coin vindictively into the palm

SETH FRIED

of some void. Then I will come crashing back to the sight of some unhappy village as it burns or the steady progress of my men through the jungle from one place to the next, the idiotic clamor of their armor through the damp.

I fire a cannon into a line of native men. Three native men strain under the weight of a large chest filled with gold, while others on either side wave their arms in supplication, half dancing their way toward our large, white tents that pulse slowly in the low breeze. It is an effort to pay tribute by men who hope to appease what they still seem to misunderstand as a greed with limits. As if there could be a set sum of gold that would suffice, as if there could be treasure enough in that pitiful chest to induce our ships back to Spain. No such sum or treasure exists. Those men suspect that the gold rattling in their ridiculous chest will stay my progress. They assume that if I am presented with it freely, I will abandon all hostility. They assume I see gold as a justification for violence, when it is exactly the opposite. I see violence as a justification for gold. Practically speaking, my purpose is not to collect gold, but to collect gold with violence. After all, unless it is gathered in a way that requires as many men and resources as possible, gold itself is useless. If gold is to be worth anything, then the act of collecting it needs to involve shipbuilders, arms makers. It needs to involve the men who grind the gunpowder, the men who pour that powder into barrels, the porters who load those barrels onto a ship. It needs to involve the men who rent those porters rooms, the men who sell those porters bread. It needs to involve the men who bake that bread, the men who grind that wheat. It needs to involve the farmers who stand grimly at the edges of those wheat fields, drenched in sweat. Gold is arbitrary. What is significant is the way in which it is seized and toward what end it drives the toil of many. If gold is going to be given up voluntarily, well, that is not sound. You see? What these weak-minded men fail to realize is that if I could take their gold without harming them, there would be no reason to want it. If I were sent here to collect the leaves off the trees, their plight would be the same. And so the cannon shot soars out over the field with a noise like ripping cloth, exploding the chest and scattering that particularly meaningless gold beyond recovery.

I am startled from my sleep. For reasons that are beyond me, I find myself standing in a field at a great distance from my men, asleep in their tents. I am holding my own sword to my throat. Wearing nothing but a helmet, I was no doubt woken by the coolness of the night air, almost a chill. Strangely, this seems to have been to my advantage, as—in my sleep—I had been working the sword against my throat. Already, there is a trickle of blood creeping along the blade. I throw the sword down, frightened—not at the possibility of having inadvertently lost my life, but at the possibility that posthumously it would have seemed an act of cowardice. I am frightened by the fact that, had it not been for the slight breeze rousing me from sleep, my legacy would have been one of weakness, and not (I look around and see that I am in fact standing among the splintered remains of that chest, that worthless tribute gold dispersed in the dirt) of strength.

In a dense wood, I kill a woman. She approaches me from behind with a curiosity that at first seems animal in its simplicity. Without a context, I must look odd. A suit of metal. My right leg turned inward. A posture suggesting weariness in a world that is otherwise a paradise. I groan slightly as I move my hand across the tree trunk. Who could approach such a bizarre creature without fear? Then again—despite my terrible appearance—perhaps I seem somehow marvelous to the woman, a spectacle. If I had turned to her without violence, maybe she would have continued to smile. Maybe she would have continued to regard me with her friendly curiosity. Yes. I am sure now. She would have tugged at my beard. She would have traced the outline of my damaged ear with her finger. She would have pressed her palm flat against my chest, slapping lightly at my breastplate and leaning in close in order to hear the dull reverberations. I would take offense at first—but before I would be able to become upset, the woman would step away. She would regard me from a short distance and then lean back in and continue to knock at my chest. Slowly, I would realize that she was admiring me, that in some pleasant way she was amused by me. She would begin to laugh, and I would laugh, too. After all, how ridiculous! Hearing her laughter, I would realize once and for all how preposterous it was. A man dressed in metal! I would begin to wonder how many different facets of my life were similarly absurd. I would sit on the ground with the woman and begin taking my armor off one piece at a time. I would hold up each piece in front of her, allowing the light to catch it, exposing swirls of dried polish and imperfections. I would hand each piece to her so that she would be able to examine it more closely. She would be visibly impressed by the design but would still wrinkle her brow, looking back and forth between me and each piece of armor, as if to say: how silly of you. After having removed it all, I would reassemble my armor and fasten it to the base of a tree, where it would stand eerily hollow and strange-looking. The woman and I would take turns throwing stones at it or rapping it with sticks, the loud clangs frightening birds from their branches. For whatever reason, my misery would not be discernable to this woman, so it would simply disappear. Without being able to exchange a single word, we would enjoy one another's company. We would be glad that we could not talk as, in silence, we would manage to prolong that childish excitement that cannot be put into words anyway, that sweet, slow grope for acquaintanceship in which every moment is the most precious failure. Instead, I strike the woman down. I kill her with a single blow. In a dense wood. Like an animal.

My men stand apart from me, gathered in a circle. They mock me as if I have already left. They take turns trying to imagine my hobbled body ravaging the woman. They make wild, grotesque faces and jerk their hips back and forth, one leg twisted and dangling. They laugh uncontrollably. They double over and drool. I unsheathe my sword, but they fail to notice. Maybe when they turn around, I will be charging to kill them. Maybe I will slice off their ears and their noses. Maybe, in the end, they will beg me for mercy. Maybe I will march them into the middle of camp and force them to eat piles of gold. Maybe they will kneel before me, bleeding, moaning, and eating gold while watching the edge of my sword as if it were the face of God. Maybe when they turn around, I will have opened a vein. Maybe they will watch me die a pale, gradual death as my blood mixes with the woman's. Maybe when they turn around, I will be gone and all that will be left is a pile of armor glittering in the dirt.

THE GREAT FRUSTRATION

· · · · · · · · · · ·

In the Garden of Eden, a cat steadies itself on a branch while quietly regarding a parrot. The air in the garden is heavy and mixed with the stink of all those animals resting below. No blood is spilled in the garden, and so the roles of most of the animals are greatly reduced. Though most of them are still, as yet, unaware of this fact. They linger in vague proximity to one another, marveling at their own bodies. The larger creatures recognize the strength in their new limbs, while others like the penguin and the guinea pig only wander clumsily from place to place, wondering whether or not they have been the object of some cruel joke. Near a small pond, the penguin waves the dull blades of its arms up at the sky, as if already protesting the existence of a dense and impractical God.

It has been said that the air in the garden is heavy with the smell of these animals. More than heavy, it is unbearable and oppressive. However, it is a smell that goes generally unnoticed by its originators, except perhaps in the form of an occasional swirl of dander, moved on a breeze not unlike the one that now rustles the fur along the cat's spine, causing it to hunker low on the branch and flatten its ears as it keeps its eyes fixed on the parrot from a respectful distance. The cat cannot help but observe the parrot with a particular interest. The cat sees it as ripe, but with what?

Below, the lion does not lie with the lamb, but neither does it tear the lamb into a thousand pieces, neither does it eat the lamb's head in a single bite, neither does it take the lamb into its jaws and, with all the force in the tremendous muscles of its neck, whip the lamb against a tree over and over again until the lamb is nothing but a skid of dripping slime on a tree trunk. Neither does the lion do any of the things that leap suddenly to mind whenever it sees the lamb. These fantasies confuse the lion because they are at once repellent and invigorating. They leave the lion with a number of questions regarding its feelings toward its fellow creatures. Why, for instance, should the lion feel a twitching in its paws when it sees the peacock? Why should the limbs of the lion jerk, as if it is being startled from a dream? Why when the peacock waddles past should the lion imagine a beautiful explosion of feathers, a cloud of dull greens and iridescent blues that pulses and churns to the rhythm of the lion's heart?

At the same time, the peacock is deeply hurt by the cold stares it receives from the lion. It wants only to be liked and the apparent disdain exhibited by the lion is more than it can bear. It moves back and forth before the lion, deliberately fanning its feathers in the hopes of being acknowledged. But the lion only presses its claws into the dirt and closes its eyes, emitting a low sound from its chest. The peacock moves toward the lion, observing it closely. The peacock wants the lion to open its eyes. It wants more than anything for the lion to admire its magnificent feathers. It strains to fan them even further. Whereas the lamb watches the peacock in disbelief. Having interpreted the gaze of the lion with far more acumen, the lamb tends to keep to the brush, sporadically poking out its head to watch the lion as if it were a great storm gathering in the distance.

The parrot is oblivious, which aggravates the cat. The parrot sits on the branch, happily looking off into the distance and occasionally stretching its wings as if it were in the middle of some imagined flight. This air of solitude and contentment is upsetting to the cat. After all, if it finds the parrot so fascinating, why shouldn't the parrot at least acknowledge its presence in the tree? This presumed haughtiness on behalf of the parrot stirs up a desire in the cat to knock it from its branch, thumping the back of its head hard enough to send it spiraling to the ground. But the inevitable sight of the parrot on the ground, so far away, would surely only fill the cat with some new anxiety. Instead, it prefers to fantasize about the possibility of placing its nose against the belly of the parrot or of opening its mouth to the parrot's throat, taking a small nip of flesh between its teeth and pinching it gently, lovingly. Some rich, phantom taste begins to fill the cat's mouth. By some mysterious impulse, the cat's jaw begins to quiver. From its throat comes a quiet chatter. Otherwise motionless, the cat remains on the branch, jealously guarding the parrot in its happiness.

And the parrot is happy. The parrot is desperate with happiness. It reveres, with a profound joy, every aspect of its life in the garden. It considers its parrothood to be an unfathomable windfall of good luck, the very thought of which causes its heart to feel overfull. Though it carries with it also a constant sense of unease. For while it holds the other animals of the garden in neighborly esteem, the parrot also regards them with a secret terror—terror in the sense that their very existence seems to serve as evidence that at some point there must have been a chance, or many chances, that the parrot could have been created as something other than a parrot. As satisfied as the parrot is with life, underlying each moment of pleasure is the frantic contemplation of all those possibilities that could have made things different. The idea that its own feathers could have been yellow instead of blue is enough to make the parrot hide its head in the crook of its wing and hold its breath, as if waiting for the alleviation of some incredible pain. The parrot cannot endure the thought of doing without any of the aspects of its existence that it likes—and it likes *all* of them. It likes the weight of its own body on the branch. It likes the sound of its own voice. Most of all, it likes flight. It prefers to spend its time flying out where the fields past the horizon are still under divine construction, where it can coast past the hard earth and look down into the sparkling void, its wings borne upward on fierce gusts of nothingness. The parrot likes to look back on the garden, shining by its own light, as it grows, slowly folding out and out. This view of the garden produces a sense of gratification so complete that the parrot feels almost burdened by it. At times, the parrot feels guilty toward the animals that are bound to the earth, toward all the other birds that are not bold enough to fly so far out. It pities them. Why should it alone have access to such wonder? The parrot senses that there is already a great inequity in the world. It takes as an example of this the poor cat that is now attempting to share its branch. It looks so awkward in the tree. And by climbing so high it is clearly trying to emulate the parrot in some way—an idea so pathetic that it sends the parrot into a deep and uncompromising despair. And look, now the cat's jaw is trembling. It sounds as if it is trying to chirp. How clearly it wants to be a bird! The parrot realizes that of all the animals in the garden, this cat, by some special intuition of its species, is alone in its ability to understand fully how unkind the parrot's advantage is. The parrot begins to understand that no matter what kind of world is created from this garden, it will be one in which birds are a plague and a misery to cats, one in which cats find themselves afraid of birds and the brilliant flapping of their wings. The indisputable nature of this fact depresses the parrot even further. The cruelty of the garden begins to wound the parrot, who otherwise adores it so much. The parrot begins to contemplate wild plans of flying out into the void and flinging itself down into it without stopping, in way of apology to all these wretched beasts chained to the earth. But, in love with life, the parrot cannot find it in its heart to act on this impulse. Instead, it only stares off into the distance, occasionally spreading its wings.

Elsewhere in the garden, a skin mite clings thoughtfully to an elephant's crotch. From that vantage, it is decidedly underwhelmed by creation. The craggy skin of the elephant stretches out beneath the mite and offers the appearance of a saggy, gray wasteland. Repulsed by such grotesque surroundings, the mite turns inward and attempts to mitigate the harshness of its existence by arriving at a kind of philosophy. Having ascended a gray valley, it looks back down into the darkness and begins to construct wild, untestable notions of the world. The mite attempts to achieve a theory that would explain the unmistakable contrast between the base nature of the world and the sweet intricacies of its own spirit. Hanging upside down from the elephant's crotch, the mite looks up at the ground, which it understands to be the firmament. It observes the gigantic bodies of the animals passing below and tries to read auguries from them, the meanings of which depend primarily on the body's size and shape, the direction from which it enters the sky and by which it exits. The mite uses these movements to guess at everything from the shape of the universe to changes in the weather, to the quiet drift of its own fortune. In its more expansive moments, it imagines that those heavenly bodies are actually living creatures. Like itself, only on some immense scale. It imagines that the roof of the firmament is actually a plain across which these creatures are able to move. It imagines the existence of such creatures as being in some way analogous to its own. Though this is where the mite's spirits begin to fail, where the mite begins to feel dizzy and without center. The mite imagines a world in which such creatures could actually exist. It imagines all the magnificent things that would be possible in such a world and feels capable of none of them.

As these thoughts take place, the elephant holds up its trunk and squints at it, as if regarding it from a great distance. It notes the complexity of its own skin, the unending ruts and crosshatches. It is faced with thoughts, which, although the exact opposite of the mite's, are no less disturbing to it.

Everywhere in the garden, there is a similar confusion and frustration. The monkey sits on the ground with its hands hanging loosely around the base of a tree. It wants to whip a stick at the back of the horse's legs. Its body seems so perfectly tuned to skitter up the tree, and it wants only for something to chase it there. The pig roots aimlessly at nothing; the frog despises the fly; the fly falls in love with the donkey and the giraffe stands awkwardly in a clearing, as if awaiting instructions.

Meanwhile, the cat creeps toward the parrot. It begins to feel impatient with its own predicament. Its lust for the parrot has grown and revealed itself as something violent. The cat sees now that it wants the parrot to droop lifelessly from its mouth, that it wants to wag the parrot back and forth until its neck pops and its beak clacks pathetically with each jerk. The muscles of the cat move toward the parrot of their own volition, as if drawn by some external force. The cat begins to understand that there are aspects of its own nature that are not under its control. This exasperates the cat. Why should it be placed in this body only to suffer some desire that is against its will? Why should it be forced to play audience to its own sickness? And if its body is not its own, then where does the cat begin? When does it start to be the cat, and not just some cooperation of limbs, motivated by compulsion and compelled irrevocably toward parrots? The cat awaits the answers to these questions.

Below, all the animals in the garden await the answers to identical questions. They wait in the midst of the very first anticipation. Their collective quiet is pulled taut, a stem straining under the weight of some great fruit. They wait for an invisible bond to be broken. They wait to be sent happily, savagely, into what's next.

THE SIEGE

· · · · · · · · · · ·

The men on the walls are all dead. The city is ravaged, but still, somehow, untaken. Imagine, if you will, a cachectic dog limping down a street littered with corpses. Corpses everywhere. The bodies of those who've succumbed to cholera. The bodies of those who, in fits of starvation, forced themselves to eat the tainted meat flung over the walls by the catapults, mangonels, and trebuchets of the impending hordes. The bodies of fighting men who, overwhelmed by the sight of our foe, the sheer size and determination and cruelty of their numbers, fled the walls in order to throw themselves onto their own swords. Imagine that spiritless dog as it sniffs and drools its way down the street piled high with the human filth amassed over the sixteen-month duration of the siege. Imagine as it nibbles off the nose from the corpse of a young girl, moves away, chomping, moves away, pausing to cough, a small tendril of mucus and blood dangling from its shriveled anus. Now imagine the same scene without a dog, because there are none. All the dogs in the city having been eaten a long, long time ago.

No, the last person naive enough to attempt keeping a dog as a pet, Wilkshire, the currier, kept a mutt and a litter of pups in his shop, sustaining them with rainwater and small bits of corpse. This was until a group of townsmen overheard a yelp through a broken window and stormed the shop, killing Wilkshire in the struggle, leaving themselves to fight over the litter and mutt, which were both soon reduced to a worthless pulp. Only old man Tuttle escaped with the runt, which he ate tauntingly from the safety of the chapel roof, lifting it from time to time, in mock benediction, toward the moon.

Things, we have to admit, are looking rather bleak.

Some of us gather around and help poison the wells for when the hordes will inevitably enter the city. There are those of us who are almost cheerful; the siege has lasted for so long that whatever happens, we'll gladly welcome something new. However, there are also those of us who know better. In the first month of the siege, the commander of the attacking forces led from a white tent. This signified that if the city were to surrender, none would be harmed. In the second month, the commander of the attacking forces led from a red tent, signifying that if the city were taken, all men bearing arms would be put to death. In the third month, enemy forces were led from a black tent, meaning that under no circumstances would any men in the city be spared. Thirteen months later, and the tent is now the color of an angry god.

* * *

Some say it's a miracle the city has lasted as long as it has. There were a few proud days in the beginning: our guards lined manfully along the walls, their armor glittering in the sun. The wide, clear sky was filled with the clatter of their spears, while the banner of our city wagged in the air with the wild enthusiasm of a fool's tongue. Though it wasn't long before the enemy's sorties to the wall, ready as they were with their countless bowmen and hundreds of mounted cheiroballistrae, reduced our forces to a pitiful pretense. Now the battlements are empty except for the occasional graybeard, who might wander up in order to move his bowels defiantly over the wall or to shake a small, withered fist.

The question now is: When will the enemy make their final escalade over the walls? This question seems to resonate within a larger question, which is: Why have they not already made their final escalade over the walls?

There are those who believe that our enemy must be preparing something unique and elaborate. There are those who expect a final stroke that will reveal our enemy's creativity to be in direct proportion to the amount of time we have, however incapably, delayed them. There are some who talk of sappers—sappers who, instead of undermining our fortifications with their deep, winding tunnels, will creep up underneath our streets, forcing up stones and finding us in the filth where we sleep, sidling up on us while we dream of hunger, removing sleek knives from their diggers' cloaks and committing us all, respectively, to our various heavens and hells.

There are some who talk of thousands upon thousands of trained birds to be released over the city. Hawks, each half the size of a man and starved to the point of madness. Others contradict this story entirely, saying it will be thousands upon thousands of a poisonous kind of butterfly, to be loosed from giant burlap sacks as the winds permit. Butterflies. It is said that, if lightly touched, they will cause the victim's skin to boil, the victim's innards to smolder like hot coals, the victim's blood to seep from under fingernails and out of eye sockets, up and out from the throat and down over the teeth from the sponge of wasted gums. It is said that at day's end, the victims of that deadly butterfly are not cooled by night's chill. Rather, touched by the fevers of the afflicted, the night burns.

We wander the city, all of us, wondering. The uncertain fears grow in us, as we expect perhaps a hand to spring from the earth beneath our feet or the sudden, violent beating of innumerable wings or the small touch of an ink-colored butterfly as it lights fraily on the noses of our upturned faces.

Some believe it's a miracle the city has lasted as long as it has, while others think it's just another possible invention of the enemy, another of their awful weapons. Waiting. The wretched, terrible weapon of waiting.

In the sixth month the women evacuated the city. One morning, without explanation, they were simply gone. We see them now from time to time, walking among the enemy camps in their new, bright dresses. From the vantage of an empty tower, some small group of us will huddle over a telescope hung through the opening of a machicolation. Watching them, we often have the feeling that our former wives, in their all too infrequent glances toward the city, are marking us with a sort of jeer.

Our wives, once familiar to us, now seem to regard the city, across the distance, with a bitterness and amused ridicule not known to us in our time with them, as if they suddenly remember nothing of the life within these walls.

Perhaps in order to ease the guilt of leaving, they have let themselves inflate some fault or imagined slight on our part, so that for every degree they loved us, they now as quickly spite us. Perhaps, because our defeat seemed unavoidable to them, they have now resolved to desire it.

Still, most of us can't help but ask ourselves if they never think of us, in their quieter moments. If they don't occasionally recall with regret some secret, truer happiness. There's no way of knowing for certain, but it's pleasant to think that their hearts might not be completely hard toward us.

As the sun comes down, we watch them walk the familiar path to some soldier's tent, to the dark, new privacies of god knows what. We watch and we wonder if they remember anything of us, if they are holding it dearly in their deepest places. Anything of us. Anything at all.

* * *

It is difficult to say from where our attackers originate or what, beyond victory, is their ultimate purpose.

They approached the city from the north, where for miles and miles extend gentle pastures, still lakes, and sporadic sprouts of forest. These eventually give way to subtle hillocks that roll on and on, swelling in places, diminishing in others, an ancient mountain range subdued and grown over with long grass and cluttered with brush. After this, there occurs a noticeable shift in the landscape, in which the earth hardens, and flora is sparser, but where the hardier creatures still roam. Nameless things, charged with their special loneliness. Then there is a large gorge, beyond which is an unknowable waste-land of cracked earth, the air filled with fits of wind and lightning without thunder. A savage place.

One would assume this to be the hearth of our foe. At any rate, it would certainly suit them. Though the real truth is that they probably come from nowhere, are motivated by nothing.

Their flag is a simple white bar against a field of black. There is no pomp. Every single soldier wears a plain hauberk, belt typically at a casual slant. The chain mail covers the entire face, revealing only the ovals of their dispassionate eyes. Their movements in battle are calm, organized, emotionless. They are swift but not eager. Pitiless but without rage.

Their purpose is to destroy us, but, having offered no reason behind this purpose, the point cannot be argued. Wherever they came from, they are the *them* and we are the *us*—and there is no choice now but a conflict, however meaningless.

In the relative calm of their camps, they stir. An empty flag is raised. A hollow horn is blown.

Though many parts of the city remain the same, it is all of it changed. Throughout the city, there might be any number of buildings or public works which, though untouched by the siege, are still somehow different from what they were before.

We pass some familiar spot and find it as it has always been. Where once there was an ash tree surrounded by loose stone, there is still an ash tree surrounded by loose stone. Where once was a crenulated archway opening into a courtyard, there is still a crenulated archway. However, around each there is a new, strange air. Difficult and close. It hangs, thick as caution, near the familiar. It flowers on either side of it, looms above it, lurks awkwardly within. Where once we were happy to sit in repose on the stoop of some shop, we are now unsettled. In such a place, once restful and welcoming, we are now suddenly seized with anxiety and a desire to flee.

As time goes on, the anxiety grows until most of us are only comfortable while frequenting those parts of the city that have already been destroyed: a beer hall with its roof puckered in by some missile. A stable reduced to a treacherous pile of splintered timbers. A statue of a noble city father, now missing a leg.

When the women evacuated the city, not one brought her children with her. This left us, the surviving men of the city, in a somewhat awkward position. That is to say, it left us, the ones accustomed to spending long days toiling outside the city, to become suddenly the sole caretakers of entire populations of tiny, dough-faced strangers.

When asked to account for their missing mothers, most of us did our best to provide our children with explanations designed to soothe them but also meant to be decidedly final: their mothers, who loved them very much, were taken by an unconfirmed illness or an unknown assailant or miscellaneous act of nature. On the other hand, there were also those of us who, still bitter over the loss of our wives, offered our children, regrettably, more inflammatory explanations: their mothers, whose opinions of them we had always held in doubt, were taken by an excruciating, disfiguring illness so contagious that they had to be hoisted over the walls with long pointed sticks; or they had been abducted by some poor, unknowing assailant or torn to pieces by a miscellaneous act of nature.

Our children viewed our initial efforts to care for them skeptically. When the food stores eventually ran out and the occasional pigeon had to be caught, the occasional rat speared desperately in the corner, their eyes exhibited the wide, damp gaze that said had their mothers been present, they never would have been forced to suffer such indignities. Admittedly, nothing about the situation is ideal. There are many of us who, without our children, would have been content to sit purposefully without food or water until our bodies weakened. However, with children came the necessity to survive. Insects had to be gathered. Rainwater collected. The bellies of city vermin opened and emptied.

* * *

There is yet another possible explanation as to why, up to this point, we have been spared. It may not be, after all, that the enemy are allowing us to linger but that, at the very breaking point of victory, our enemy are allowing *themselves* to linger.

In fact, all reports from the wall suggest that the lines of circumvallation have been growing settled as of late. More and more dirt has been displaced for earthen bunkers within the trenches. Often, in the distance, we catch sight of what appear to be men shaving, men hanging laundered undergarments on impromptu lines and bathing in shallow bronze tubs. Further back, slightly more permanent fixtures are beginning to appear: A wooden mess hall. A modest officer's club.

This, to say the least, is a troubling sign.

With the enemy having the benefit of our wives and we the benefit of our children, it becomes clear that this siege could become not a simple matter of months or even years but a matter of generations. If the enemy continues to settle, who's to say that the siege won't eventually become just a city encircling a lesser city? It begins with a few small buildings and a casual nickname, arrived at by a pair of drunken captains on some invaders' holiday: Siege Town. A trader's post might be added, a few shops established and, a century later, it's a thriving capital by the name of Siegton or Sigton or some other unintentional contraction. And though eventually the siege might not be actively practiced, the lesser city taken in by the greater, it would, however, in one way or another, be absorbed into this new city's culture, sublimated into any number of its customs. The fact of the siege would live on in some elusive metaphor. It would affect the way our descendants talk or the way they think about talking. It would change the way they think or the way they think about thinking. In whatever language that is taken up, perhaps, the word for *desired* might be the same as the word for *conquered*. The word for *correct*, the same as *victory*. *Incorrect*: *defeat*. There might be no word for *weak* due to the presence of the word *unnecessary*. A young girl in love might be described as a *toppled citadel*. A newborn baby as being *without helmet*. Two people in disagreement might both be said to have a *position*, which through argument could either be *attacked* or *defended*. Citizens of that city, overwhelmed with a multitude of tasks, might choose to describe themselves as feeling *bombarded*. Flowers, no longer given in *bouquets*, might then find themselves in *quivers*.

Time would exhaust itself forward, and this siege, the great sadness of our time on earth, would send out an unending ripple, creating an impossible legacy—while we, the surviving men of the city, would fade to nothing. Our side of this conflict, our thoughts and hopes and fears, would all serve as just another aborted path of fate and its lazy, meandering plot.

Of course, for all our complaints, some might call us cowards. Why, after all, were we not among the fighting men on the walls? Why, when our wives abandoned us, did we do nothing? Or why do we now allow our children to suffer in the shadow of our own passivity? Why, even if we could by no means break the lines of the enemy, do we not, if just on the most basic principle, go out from the walls to meet them, dying honorably?

To these questions we answer only that there are many kinds of courage, ours being a quiet and personal type.

When approached with a force of change beyond compromise, this force not merely the enemy in question but destiny itself, we answer softly, to whatever its agenda: no. Even if we have no means or intention of resisting it, even if our only course is to maintain our course, even if our unwillingness to placate yoked to our unwillingness to defy accomplishes nothing, it doesn't matter. Our purpose is to remain true. To what? It doesn't matter. For how long? Indefinitely.

That is our kind of courage and in the act of fighting, we would lose it.

Our courage is akin to patience. No matter what kind of world is created for us, the mind will always be large enough to give refuge, and so our visions of the world will always have their place.

And what of our enemy's kind of courage? Certainly it will bring them victory as an army, but what of each man? City after city will be defeated, victory after victory will accrue, but eventually the lines will advance too far into some district intended for future conquest: a clot of wounded men stands in the middle of a frozen river, helplessly watching the charge of some wild, frigid race whose axes in hand and beards flagging behind them spell out, clearly, the end. What of each man?

What does that type of courage win him in the end? To that man personally, it wins him the greatest loss of all, but a loss which, to the forces he served, is so small as to be completely unweighable.

Each and every one of our enemies will die, just like us. All they've done is attach themselves to a type of courage that will outlive them, and if that courage is the real courage and our courage is not, then so be it: We are, every one of us, cowards, and our enemies are all distinctly brave men.

Then again . . .

Then again, maybe, if we had it to do over again, there would be a few things we would choose to do differently.

Our children, feeling playful, kick rubble to one another down the street; feeling thirsty, stand watching the sky, praying for a storm cloud to gather. Do we wish we had fought on the walls? No. But maybe if we had fallen asleep with our arms draped lovingly across our wives, their leaving would have woken us, allowing us to say something, even if it were only good-bye. Maybe if we knew our children better, it would have been easier to turn eating a rat into a kind of game. In short, maybe there's more we could have risked.

But what's happened has happened. The city is ravaged yet still, somehow, untaken. Some of us gather around and help poison the already fetid wells for when the hordes will inevitably . . . There's not much left to be done. Keep the children off the corpses, the corpses off the walkways. Watch the walls. Watch the walls. Wait for the possible breach. A dull rumble and burst of men through the city.

Outside, troops wander the lines encircling the city in different states of preparedness. At various points are positioned officers on horseback. Absently, a hoof is raised and lowered. A mane is shaken. Each officer sits casually, hands loose on the reins, scanning the sky for some unknown sign that we know may never come.

THE FRENCHMAN

. . . .

In the seventh grade, I starred in a play written by my school's gym teacher. That year, Mr. Whitley had bullied the school board into letting him teach a section of drama so that they would be forced to raise his salary on a technicality. Whitley told those of us in his fourth period Theater Arts class that he had written the play because drama was in his goddamned blood. But we all knew that he had only slapped it together over the Columbus Day weekend in order to assuage accusations made by the PTA that he was unqualified to teach drama.

For those of us in his class, participation in the play was mandatory. Titled *Death Mansion*, the flyers made by Whitley had promoted it as "a story of international intrigue"— whereas the script itself had my classmates and I attempting to solve a murder mystery while unwittingly espousing Whitley's shockingly intolerant worldview.

My character was named Louis the Frenchman. My costume consisted of a pencil-thin moustache, candy cigarette, loud pink scarf, and matching beret. Whenever there was talk of the murderer striking again, the script had me duck behind Jerome the Former Slave and shout "I surren-dare!" At other times, I was to leer dramatically at Consuela el Tapas, the fiery Spanish maiden. I was to grab at her waist and pretend to drool. In what was intended to be the first big laugh of the night, when Fräulein Deutchstrudel asked her guests whether she could get them anything, the script had me leap up and shout, "I want more wiiiiiiiiiiiine!" Instead of laughter, this line was greeted with the sound of the parents in the audience shifting in their seats, fidgeting in collective discomfort.

In the public outrage that followed our class's one and only performance of *Death Mansion*, the front page of *The Hancock Evening News* featured a picture of me at that very moment. In the photograph, I'm standing at center stage with my arms thrown out like a French Al Jolson. My beret is pushed back at a jaunty angle on my head, and my face is contorted in such a way as to telegraph to the viewer that the accent I am affecting is the product of a joyful ignorance. Next to me in the picture is a girl in a conical hat, who is looking off uncertainly into the audience. The headline reads: *Sacrebleu! Teacher Fired Over Hate Play*.

Tony Goldman's family ended up filing a lawsuit against the school district. Tony had played the part of Jerome, and his appearance in blackface had been one of the lightning rod issues surrounding the play. Susan Wilson's family filed a similar suit. She was the girl standing next to me on the front page of *The Hancock Evening News*. Drawing on Whitley's confused understanding of the Far East, Susan had been given the costume of a Cambodian farmer, and yet her character was referred to in the script several times as "but a lowly geisha." After both the Goldmans and the Wilsons won their suits, the parents of almost every student involved in the play began meeting with attorneys regarding the psychological damage that had been done to their children by being forced to take part in it.

However, my parents were among the few not to do so. They found my participation in *Death Mansion* to be so humiliating that it never occurred to them to pursue the issue publicly. All of us in Whitley's play were too young and too uninformed to know how offensive any of it was. In rehearsals, we had all been equally amused by the play. But while we were on stage, the other students began to notice the stony reception that we were receiving. After a while, they gradually toned their performances down and began to deliver their lines in an embarrassed, perfunctory fashion. There was an untaught decency in them which allowed them to understand that something about what was happening on stage was unacceptable. I, on the other hand, remained completely oblivious, and spent the duration of *Death Mansion* chewing the scenery. Due to my ad-libbing alone, the play overshot the runtime estimated in the program by twenty minutes. Apropos of nothing, I would announce to the other characters on stage, "Een Pair-ee we dance like zis!" Then I would launch into a paroxysm of dance that, in the infinite silence of that auditorium, must have seemed to last forever.

I was so caught up in the ecstasy of my ridiculous performance that I failed to notice that there was no applause during the curtain call. As the event broke up and parents began to escort their children home, I noticed Susan Wilson crying in the arms of her mother. At the time, I assumed that this was a response to Susan feeling the same overwhelming sensation of catharsis that I felt after having given so much of myself on the stage.

As I searched for my parents in the school's auditorium, it was difficult for me to imagine the amount of praise that my performance would inspire in them. They were notoriously easy to please. When I was nine years old, I wore jean shorts to a family function and accidentally had explosive diarrhea on my aunt Rebecca's kitchen floor. Later that day, my parents had complimented me—in earnest—on having had the presence of mind to do it in a room with a linoleum floor. But when I found my parents in the crowd after Whitley's play, they didn't say a word. My mother threw her coat over me while my father lifted me over his shoulder and carried me out to the parking lot in a nervous half run. As we drove off, my mother regarded the school as if it were on fire.

Once we were home, my father told me that I was to never bring up Whitley's play again under pain of being disowned. He made me throw out my Louis the Frenchman costume, and for at least that first night I fought back tears over the bitter knowledge that my parents were insane. It wasn't until

Whitley was fired that I began to realize just how universal their reaction was.

There were several other photographs on page six of *The Hancock Evening News* in which I was shown cowering in an exaggeratedly comic fashion behind Tony Goldman in blackface. Another showed me addressing Susan Wilson's Asian character while pulling at my eyes in imitation of an epicanthic fold. In yet another, I was goose-stepping behind Fräulein Deutchstrudel. The other students looked frightened in the photographs, whereas I looked completely at ease with everything I was doing. Looking at those pictures, it was as if the entire play had been my idea.

Though my parents refused to take part in the legal circus that followed the play, my father did place a few angry phone calls to the editor of *The Hancock Evening News* warning him not to print any more photographs of me. But by then the damage had been done. Everyone involved agreed that it was unreasonable to blame a child for the faults of a forty-seven-year-old gym teacher. Nevertheless, the idiotic verve with which I had carried out my role had been hard to ignore. In the faces of my teachers and classmates, I saw that the ignorance I had inadvertently expressed on stage was now being regarded as an immutable part of who I was.

After Whitley's play, even the younger, more willfully optimistic teachers were reluctant to call on me. Even the students who enjoyed telling racist jokes in the cafeteria understood that, because they had never had an example of their bigotry published in a newspaper, they therefore occupied the moral high ground. The memory of the play itself faded within a few weeks, but the stigma of it remained attached to me for years. From that point on, my life became defined by a stubborn and overwhelming sense of shame.

My father eventually lifted his prohibition against mentioning the play. Throughout high school, it was even a running joke between us. Whenever I did something particularly thoughtless he would call me Louis, at which point I would laugh and apologize for whatever offense had revived the old joke. There was no way for him to know how much it actually bothered me to be reminded of Louis the Frenchman, or how much I wished that we had stayed true to his original decree that we never mention Whitley's play again.

Even now, I am often afraid that those photographs from *The Hancock Evening News* will somehow resurface in my adult life, and I will be forced to answer for them. Of course, this fear is irrational. Those pictures are now almost two decades old. No one would even be able to recognize me as that twelve-year-old boy, dressed as a flamboyant Frenchman. But the small chance that someone could recognize me is enough to keep that fear alive.

Perhaps my biggest concern is that my wife would find out about it. She's originally from the Netherlands, and though the entirety of Dutch culture somehow managed to remain safely off of Whitley's radar during the writing of *Death Mansion*, I would still be humiliated to have her learn about my participation in a play that so willfully misunderstood other peoples.

After all, I've seen waiters furrow their brows at my wife's accent, as if they're owed an explanation. I've seen grocery store clerks make her feel stupid on the rare occasion that she flubs her English. I've seen television commercials and children's shows portray the country where her grandparents are buried as a cartoon landscape of windmills and wooden shoes. And while she is too even-tempered and reflexively happy to let these images bother her for long, I can still recognize that for a moment they do, that it frustrates her to see that place—filled with all the indescribable memories of her youth—reduced to something offensively cute.

There are times when these different forms of insensitivity pile up one after the other, so that by the end of the day it is clear that she is struggling with a deep sense of exclusion. On such nights, I'll often hear her talk in her sleep. These are short episodes—memories of when she first began to live in the States—in which she is attempting to remember a word in English that is constantly eluding her. In these episodes, she is addressing dry cleaners and asking strangers for directions—all those nerve-racking first interactions. Her voice is always apologetic and full of unease. If I can anticipate one of these episodes coming on, I will wake her in order to spare her the anxiety. But if I don't pay attention, I might be startled by the sudden sound of my wife trying to remember how to say *dinner roll* in English, as she relives some incident in a restaurant seven years ago.

Hearing her like this, I tend to think back on Louis the Frenchman and feel the pangs of that old shame. The notion that anyone would make a person as intelligent and kind and generous of spirit as my wife feel unwelcome or out of place fills me with an outrage that is directed only at myself.

Though there are also certain moments of grace. When I wake her, she always knows that she has been talking in her sleep. She will ask me what it was this time, and I will explain that she was trying to get the waiter to bring her more rolls. Then she will say the word triumphantly—*rolls!*—before promptly falling back to sleep.

In moments like that—my wife having been comforted by the knowledge that she is in bed with her husband—I ask myself: When did I start to know better? When did I start to become the man who deserves her? When did the massive shortcomings of my youth become a door that I walked through? In my mind, I see that photograph on the front page of *The Hancock Evening News*, my arms outspread in the full flower of my stupidity. I try to tell myself that it was happening in that instant, even before I understood.

LIE DOWN AND DIE

. . . .

My father was shot and killed the day after I was born. He was in St. Louis, Missouri, at the time and I am forced to assume that things did not go well for him there. I am forced to assume a great deal about my father—that he was tall, that he shaved against the grain, or that his death was tragic and undeserved—and while I have never been one to give in to superstitions, I am also forced to assume that somehow he knew he would never live long enough to see me alive.

For instance, he took me to a baseball game when I was still in the womb. There is a photograph of my mother leaning back uncomfortably in Tiger Stadium, a baseball cap propped at a careful angle on her stomach. This seems, to me, the act of a man who had serious doubts concerning his ability to survive the nine months it would take for his son to be born.

My mother never explained why my father had been shot or by whom, which even as a child I regarded as strange—a strangeness which was complicated by the fact that when I was thirteen years old my mother was abducted on an unannounced, impromptu trip to Niagara Falls and was never seen again.

My family was full of stories like that: dubious suicides, sudden disappearances, the police always suspecting foul play. An uncle would vanish only to be found mangled in farm equipment miles away from home; a cousin would run away, turning up weeks later with her wrists slit in the cargo hull of a ship bound for South America. It was as if our family tree had been written in invisible ink, names and branches disappearing as quickly as they were written.

Even things that were attached to our family by the simple means of possession seemed doomed: pets would burst into flames; appliances, fresh out of the box, would eerily fail to work.

I remember watching my aunt Loyola one summer afternoon as she plugged a brand-new blender into the wall of her cream-colored kitchen and held down the button marked PULSE. She listened intently to the unnatural whirs and clicks as the blades refused to spin and then, suddenly, as if the hum of the blender's failing was the sound that marked all our dooms, she burst into tears.

Six months later she was struck and killed by a Buick in the parking lot of Blessed Sacrament Church after Saturday night mass.

These deaths, of course, were difficult to grow up around and to this day when I leave my apartment it is not without a certain amount of consternation. I see vans with tinted windows, crop threshers and wood chippers placed inexplicably in the middle of busy streets; there are suspicious sounds, angry-looking strangers, reckless people everywhere, all bent toward some yet-unknown harm—and at these times, when I see the moment coming, streetlights flickering out the second I step under them, the moment of my certain, untimely death, I tend to think of my mother and father in terms of fate and possibilities.

I think about the possibility of a foul ball hitting my mother in the stomach that day at Tiger Stadium and the subsequent miscarriage. I think about my father dodging the bullet meant for him in St. Louis and beating his assailant within an inch of his life. I think about my mother going over the Falls in a barrel, narrowly escaping abduction and explaining her story to rescuers after being fished out of the foaming waters and pried out of the barrel; I see her, standing on the deck of a stunned ferry, damp and breathless.

My mind drifts and the moment passes and then I'm never dead—and all at once the idea that the world is a history of sad and preposterous deaths seems almost comforting.

What happens after that can be different. Sometimes after-ward the moon looks big or there's the faraway sound of a train or I might hear a dog bark or locusts so loud it hurts.

THE SCRIBES' LAMENT

· · · · · · · · · · ·

All manuscripts of Anglo-Saxon poetry are deplorably inaccurate, evincing, in almost every page, the ignorance of an illiterate scribe, frequently (as was the monastic custom) copying from dictation; but of all Anglo-Saxon manuscripts that of *Beowulf* may, I believe, be conscientiously pronounced the worst . . .

—Benjamin Thorpe,
The Anglo-Saxon Poems of Beowulf,
the Scôp or Gleeman's Tale, and the Fight at Finnesburg

Brother Ælfric entered the chapter house that morning carrying a straw dummy. He explained to us that the dummy was a thane and then climbed up onto a stool and began biting at its midsection. He stayed perched atop the stool even after the dummy lost its rather pale resemblance to a thane, after it was eviscerated and its straw remains lay scattered about the floor. He shouted out the details of a battle in a mead hall, and we all did our best to write them down.

He lost his balance just as he was in the middle of a particularly involved image regarding the joints of the mead hall as they strained to contain the battle. He fell headfirst into a cluster of empty writing desks, his face bouncing off one on the way down, producing a sound that was, perhaps by design, epic in scope.

He remained motionless beneath the desks for a moment before rising up in a great clatter, lifting his arms over his head with his hands held in imitation of claws and roaring at the desks as if expecting them to flee in terror. This sort of thing would have gone on all morning if it weren't for the fact that Brother Wigbert—a young man known for his rather sensitive disposition—inadvertently dropped his quill and then began fumbling clumsily to retrieve it. When Ælfric saw that one of his scribes had stopped writing, he let out a tremendous howl and charged at Wigbert, who, propelled by instinct, began to run for his life.

The two proceeded to make a circuit around the chapter house, Wigbert filling that wide-open space with his boyish yelps. Extremely tall and thin, Wigbert was a stark contrast to Ælfric, who was stout with muscular arms and a low, round stomach. With his long stride, Wigbert was at first able to keep a fair amount of distance between himself and his pursuer. But Ælfric was strangely fast, and every so often Wigbert would steal a glance back toward the dreadful sight of that seemingly crazed man as he steadily closed the distance.

In pursuit, Ælfric remained in character. In his bearing he was every bit that grim-guest—he had many epithets for the creature—that sin-herder, Grendel. He broke from this only when giving us instruction.

"Write down the specifics of this man's gait," he said, while continuing to chase Wigbert. "And also, his death-cry."

At this, Wigbert began to run at an even more frenzied pace.

In his blind dash to escape Ælfric, he tripped over one of the toppled writing desks and fell to the floor. There, he whimpered quietly for a moment before a small trickle of blood from his nose set him off weeping unabashedly.

Ælfric rolled Wigbert onto his back and straddled him.

"Observe," he said, "as a Spear-Dane is disemboweled."

Ælfric pressed his fists down onto Wigbert's stomach, and then quickly jerked them away, lifting them up so that they could be more easily observed. By some sleight of hand, his fists were suddenly filled with the same paleyellow straw that had served as the flesh for his thane dummy. Wigbert seemed to regard the raised fists of Ælfric as if they actually did contain his viscera. He screamed. It was a tormented sound that he sent plaintively up to the high, vaulted ceiling of the chapter house just before fainting. Pleased with this, Ælfric turned to make sure that we had all been paying attention. When he saw our sober note-taking, he smiled and threw both fistfuls of straw up into the air, declaring the day's narration complete.

Brother Ælfric was—the abbot had explained to us shortly before his arrival—an exceptional scholar. We had always equated scholarship with silence and discipline, and so we expected from Ælfric an exceptional amount of silence, discipline. According to the abbot, we were to work closely with Ælfric to aid him in the creation of works that would be to the glory of God.

We had been chosen to assist him because of our intelligence and our hearty, but not immodest, curiosity. We were not like those scribes who wrote down words without knowing their meaning. We copied manuscripts with a keen understanding, one word leading logically into the next. Great lovers of language, we recognized the same look of fulfillment in one another's faces as we worked, an abiding gratitude to the Lord for having given us access to the world of words, their firm and apprehensible meaning. After all, wasn't that the foundation of our faith? It was the word of God that we followed. It was the word of God that instructed us and which propagated all goodness in the world.

We had at first been eager to learn whatever the renowned Ælfric could teach us, but the dignified scholar we had anticipated ended up being not so much a servant of God as an act of Him.

None of us enjoyed Ælfric's method of dictation, but it was what followed that we dreaded most. After whatever madness had taken place that day, it was our task to compose a collaborative draft of the story that Ælfric had just told us. The only variation in this routine was whatever violence Ælfric chose to demonstrate and whatever part of the story—the scenes always jumbled and hopelessly out of order—he chose to narrate.

But the trouble was this: there were eleven of us scribes and the individual sets of notes that we took during Ælfric's dictation were always radically different. Even if we could agree to use what we had observed during the flight of Wigbert through the chapter house in order to describe a Spear-Dane fleeing the monster Grendel, we were still at odds as to what such a description should look like. We would write, "Spear-Dane, face _____ with fear." Then we would all consult our notes and erupt with adjectives.

"Pale!"

"Dark!"

"Stubborn!"

"Tawny!"

If we attempted to describe the Spear-Dane's gait as he ran, we would encounter a dozen similes which were conflicting and, to each scribe's thinking, definitive. The Spear-Dane ran like a startled hare. Like a powerful stag. Like a newborn colt. Like a wounded bird attempting to resume flight. By inserting all these into a single draft, we would wind up with a chimera of a Spear-Dane, an amorphous creature made up of horse haunches and bent wings. But what was the point of describing a man fleeing a monster if, in doing so, you could no longer distinguish one from the other? And any effort to rule out one simile in favor of another would only result in heated, unfriendly arguments.

Each description was unique to a single person's point of view, and so our arguments for and against each quickly became personal. It was not possible to proceed otherwise. If we were questioned about the way we described Ælfric's pursuit of Wigbert in our notes, the only thing for any of us to say in our own defense was that we had written what we had seen. In this sense, there was no way for any of us to establish the quality of an observation without simply referencing the observation itself. So, the only way to debate the quality of a description was to direct one's arguments toward the quality of the man responsible for it. Having lived in close quarters with one another for the majority of our adult lives, one can imagine the ugliness that would tend to result from this style of debate.

During an argument over Brother Edgar's account of Wigbert's so-called death-cry, Brother Aswalt brought up the unfortunate incident six years prior when Edgar had farted during vespers. In rebuttal, Edgar lashed out at Brother Albert, whose morning erections—Edgar announced—were often unmistakable beneath his robes. Accusations and unfavorable remembrances of this sort went around the room several times until eventually a sandal was thrown and somebody shoved someone, who, in turn, shoved someone else.

A brawl would have ensued if one of us hadn't come up with the idea to have Wigbert chased around the chapter house again. With the noted exception of Wigbert, everyone agreed that this would allow us to re-observe the fact of Wigbert being chased and thus vindicate the correct observation.

Though nowhere near as frightening as Ælfric, Edgar managed to do a credible job of scaring Wigbert, who, for his part, looked every bit as terrified as he had during his first bolt through the chapter house. By a fortunate coincidence, Wigbert tripped over the same writing desk he had failed to notice earlier that morning. Our restaging of the event was incredibly successful, and it was clear by the way we all applauded when Wigbert again screamed and fainted that we assumed the problem of our conflicting observations to have been finally solved. But as soon as Wigbert was helped up and led back to his seat, where he then lowered his head and refused to participate for the rest of the day, we fell into disagreement as to whose observation had just been vindicated.

The following day, Ælfric was dressed in a dragon costume. Though three times the height of a man and twice as long, it was not so much a costume as it was a large structure, which Ælfric inhabited for the greater part of the morning. Unlike Ælfric's thane dummy, the construction of the dragon was rather impressive. Whenever the costume moved, strings would raise and lower its drooping burlap feet in broad gestures meant to indicate a beast's way of walking. At the same time, some mechanism beneath the structure would set the dragon into an unnaturally fluid locomotion. Ælfric was somehow able to control the movement of the dragon's neck, the direction of its head, and even the opening and closing of its jaws. After exploring the space of the chapter house thoroughly, the dragon came to an abrupt stop, and then seemed to regard us with its large, charcoal-smear eyes.

"Describe me," it said. "Write down the specifics of my lizard-flesh."

The movement of the beast's jaws matched its words, but its voice seemed to ring out from its stomach. We understood this to be an indication of Ælfric's position within the monster. Though occasionally we would hear him climb a small flight of stairs leading up the dragon's throat, at which point he would deliver a particularly long speech from the dragon's mouth or else throw out a few armfuls of straw in a limp, pathetic imitation of fire.

The operation of the costume must have been strenuous work, and the confines of the dragon's stomach rather warm. We assumed as much because we perceived that Ælfric was naked inside the costume. Whenever he ascended the beast's throat, we would hear the instantly recognizable sound of bare feet slapping up the steps. Also, most of the dragon's skin had been fashioned from old grain sacks that Ælfric had appropriated from one of the small cellars beneath the refectory. In the places where the sacks were worn, we eventually and quite unintentionally began to catch glimpses of the occasional bare shoulder or pale, white buttock.

Against those same worn places in the sackcloth, Ælfric would every so often press an inquisitive eye in order to observe our progress. We were as frightened at the prospect of having Ælfric make an example of us while inside his costume as we were of having him do so, in his present condition, while outside it, and so we continued to write with an exaggerated diligence.

Wigbert even took the precaution of fastening his quill in place with a length of string wound around his index finger. This method served him well throughout the morning, but Ælfric had been so pleased with Wigbert's performance on the previous day that, quill-strap notwithstanding, it seemed inevitable that he would be singled out again.

From inside the costume, Ælfric spoke of the dragon's rage, which had been brought about by the theft of a golden cup. Ælfric demonstrated this rage by having the dragon throw out several fire blasts, that is, damp armfuls of straw. Ælfric then shifted the focus of his narration back to the story's hero, Beowulf, now an aging king. And as he spoke of that great leader and shaker of spears, whose deeds were known throughout the land and who was the only man who could oppose the dragon, he very slowly—with the sound of gears steadily cranking—began to point the dragon toward Wigbert.

The battle that proceeded was stranger and more difficult to describe than any of us could have anticipated. Though it was not the fact that Wigbert received a severe beating from Ælfric's dragon that made it strange. Nor was it the fact that Ælfric managed to snatch up Wigbert in the dragon's jaws, waving him viciously in the air over our heads. As remarkable as it was to behold—Wigbert being dangled and shaken, Wigbert being flung across the chapter house, Wigbert being knocked to the floor—this part of the battle was more or less predictable. Wigbert was a coward and Ælfric was in command of a dragon. When we saw Wigbert drooping helplessly from the dragon's mouth, the whole scene had an air of common sense about it. But what made it strange was that in the contest between Beowulf and the dragon, at certain points, Wigbert, as Beowulf, was supposed to be winning.

The dragon would set Wigbert down and then react to blows that were presumably being delivered by Wigbert, who was not participating at all, but only cowering beneath his adversary in a sort of wounded confusion. The sight of the dragon being driven back by the imagined attacks of a man who was simply doing his best to maintain consciousness created an extremely perverse dynamic. These episodes in which the dragon pretended to be defending itself seemed even more cruel and humiliating to Wigbert than the savage beatings that both preceded and followed them.

All told, the spectacle of Wigbert fighting the dragon was incredibly complex. Considering how difficult it had been for us to put into words Wigbert's and Ælfric's simple exchange a day earlier, the task of producing a collaborative draft based on this exchange would have proven impossible.

The problem of our conflicting descriptions continued to trouble us. Since words were the foundation of our faith, it was important that they adhere to the things they were meant to describe in a way that was uniform. But if the observation of a single phenomenon—like Wigbert being chased or, in this instance, mauled by a dragon—inspired different descriptions from different individuals, it raised the concern that words were not a vessel for truth but opinion. This thought disturbed us immensely, and none of us had any desire to explore it further.

It was for this reason that we came up with a plan to help us avoid this consideration altogether and resolve our difficulties in composing a collaborative draft. Before we arrived at the chapter house that morning, we selected at random a lead note-taker, who would be responsible for making an initial set of observations. It was agreed that the man to the left of the lead note-taker would make an exact copy of those notes. The man to the left of the second would do the same, and so on, until the end of Ælfric's narration, when we would simply combine our identical notes.

Our desks in the chapter house were arranged in a half circle, with each at just the right distance from the next to allow us a clear view of what our neighbor was writing. This plan was ideal because it made use of our special skill of copying manuscripts. Furthermore, we knew that it would give us all the appearance of working attentively during Ælfric's dictation. We even had the foresight to position Wigbert at the end, so that if Ælfric chose to make use of him, the chain would remain unbroken. Watching Wigbert as he was flung again and again across the chapter house, we all silently congratulated each other on our collective intuition.

When the battle between Wigbert and the dragon was finished, the dragon having been somehow vanquished, we heard Ælfric pull one last, groaning lever that caused the dragon to fall slowly to its side. Wigbert, sobbing in relief, began to race back to his desk. However, as the dragon fell, it became clear that the towering apparatus of the costume was about to fall directly on top of him. He managed to get just within arm's reach of his desk before the dragon's head crashed down over him, driving him through the stone floor of the chapter house like a nail into soft wood. From there, Wigbert and the dragon's head, which had been separated from the rest of the costume in the impact, fell down into an old storage pit, which had been built over in one of the abbey's countless renovations.

Moments later, the only sound in the chapter house was of Ælfric fumbling with something inside the toppled dragon. He then emerged from the creature's belly wearing a freshly donned loincloth. His face was covered in perspiration and radiant with exertion. Very nearly out of breath, he told us to start work on our draft and left the room.

We all gathered around the crater in the floor of the chapter house, where we began calling down into the surprising depth of the pit and asking Wigbert if he was alive. He did not answer us directly, but we heard him moan quietly to himself. Then, in a confused tone, he began to recite the Book of Job. We were unable to see if he was injured because the severed head of the dragon covered his entire person—all except for his right hand, which had been driven up through one of the dragon's eyes, and which, miraculously, still bore its quill.

With Wigbert in the pit, there was a delay in our usual proceedings. While we had no difficulty removing the dragon's head, it took quite some time for us to rescue Wigbert. He had received a nasty blow to the head and was consequently out of his mind. Whenever we lowered the rope down to him, he would simply bat it away and begin to giggle like a young girl deflecting a compliment. On several occasions, he deliriously grabbed hold of the rope only to let go after we had hoisted him two thirds of the way up.

When we finally managed to get him out—securing the rope around Byrhtnoth's waist and lowering him down to grab Wigbert—we saw that, though still not in his right mind, he was for the most part unharmed. We celebrated with a series of loud cheers in such a frenzy of good feeling that for a moment we lost track of Wigbert, who, as soon as he had been set down on his own two feet, had begun to wander about the chapter house speaking gibberish. Fortunately, we came to our senses in enough time to stop him just as he was beginning to climb back down into the pit.

None of us were particularly fond of Wigbert, but we were gladdened by his rescue. We saw it as evidence of our ability to pull together and bring even the most troublesome task to an agreeable end. Emboldened by this small victory, we turned our attention to the composition of the day's story. We picked up our various sets of notes which, on account of our clever strategy, we fully expected to be identical. Albert wrote, "The dragon was _____." We all consulted our notes, and then shouted out—in gleeful unison—completely different adjectives.

Stunned, we read each set of notes in relation to the next. The second was a slight variation on the first. The third was a variation on the second. By the time we reached the fourth, it was all unrecognizable. We looked at one another in disbelief.

How could this have happened? Unless—it was Aswalt who first suggested it, looking down at his notes as if they were stirring up huge and cataclysmic thoughts—the act of copying a text was itself interpretive. If this were true, then it bore implications regarding not just the work we were in the process of doing for Ælfric, but all the work we had ever done as scribes.

The sense of satisfaction that we had always derived from copying manuscripts was that we believed if we were given the same text to copy as one of our peers, the two copies produced by us would be identical. But the more we discussed our predicament, the more we realized that while we might set out with the intention of staying true to the original text, our minds—racing from one word to the next—would unwittingly begin to express all their hidden preferences and opinions. For the first time, we saw that our efforts were not interchangeable, that each of our experiences in copying a text was as unique and unverifiable as our descriptions of Wigbert being chased through the chapter house.

A great loneliness followed this line of thought. If our existence as scribes was unverifiable, then so was our existence as Christians. Worse, as human beings. The fact that we had up until that point referred to one another as *Brother* was suddenly as ridiculous as the fact that we had once referred to the Scriptures as *truth*. How was any notion of brotherhood possible when no experience could be shared? How was any notion of truth possible when all we knew of reality was derived from our own feeble observations? In the end, it was not just our failure as scribes that we were dealing with, but the failure of words to penetrate the solitude of human experience.

Our discussion on this subject gradually faded into an embarrassed silence, and, given the weight of our realization, we did not resume speaking until the implicit and unanimous decision had been made for each of us to lay the blame on every man present except himself. We picked up one another's notes and began to ridicule them with all the contempt that our newfound uncertainty had afforded us. Even though we knew our position was not a matter of our individual errors but of a seemingly unavoidable disillusionment, we treated each other's efforts from that day as if they were the cause of all our troubles. We shouted at one another violently, our voices filled with self-righteous anger. Even Wigbert, who had curled up beneath his desk, began to make unpleasant noises in his sleep.

ANIMALCULA: A Young Scientist's Guide to New Creatures

· · · · · · · · · · ·

I.	DAWSON	VIII.	HALIFITE
II.	ELDRIT	IX.	KIRKLIN
III.	KESSEL	X.	KAYLITE
IV.	MELITE	XI.	LASAR
V.	BARTLETT	XII.	PAGLUM
VI.	BASTROM	XIII.	ADORNUS
VII.	PRINCIPLES OF OBSERVATION	XIV.	PERIGITE
		XV.	SONITUM

* * *

— DAWSON —

It would seem odd to refer to an animalculum as being beautiful. All animalcula are so small that, though they are all around us, it is as if they exist on a different plane than our own, one impossibly distant and foreign, against which it would hardly make sense to apply any standard of aesthetic judgment familiar to us. And yet, it cannot be denied that the dawson is exquisitely beautiful.

It should be clarified that—in this context—the term *beautiful* is not being used as it might otherwise be by some exuberant naturalist, wishing to impress upon you his opinion that the mating ritual of desert warthogs is actually an elegant dance or that your typical lichen is as good an example of balance and cool, reciprocal quantities as any modern painting. It is common for scholars to speak of their disciplines in terms that are overly romantic. A mathematician will refer to a particularly complex problem as if it were a symphony, while a herpetologist will inevitably describe a corn snake shedding its own skin as being somehow erotic. However, it is not in this sad, bookish fashion that the dawson can be considered beautiful. The dawson is in no way similar to some desperate marriage between fungus and alga or a snake losing itself in the dirt or tusked pigs humping heartlessly among the dunes. No. Unlike with the naturalist, the mathematician, and the herpetologist, it is not out of a desire to make their field seem more dynamic that the dawson is admired by all those who study it. The truth is actually much more shameful than that.

Attempting to word the situation as delicately as possible: the dawson is beautiful in the way that one person might be beautiful to another. Though it is only a small, amorphous creature, its movements are charming and somehow endearing. At times, its movements are—for lack of a more nuanced term—sexy. In the same way that the chance sight of a young woman's ponytail bobbing in the distance, the shape of that movement, might suddenly fill a person with an inexplicable sense of longing—in the same way that the sight of a young man pushing his sleeves up and over his forearms might awaken in another person unimagined desires, so will the dawson fascinate those that observe it.

The qualities of this creature, which so stubbornly resists an objective description, are unlikely to be lost on you—you, in the eager flower of your youth—as you begin to examine it for the first time. In all likelihood, you will admire its beauty from the onset, but what will begin life as a vague appreciation will slowly turn into a much deeper affection, a pure admiration of the creature in every possible sense.

It is for this reason that many young scientists, such as yourselves, have begun to dedicate their lives to the study of the dawson. Many university libraries are being overwhelmed with long, maudlin dissertations on the subject, most of which tend to read like distraught love letters. A walking tour of any academic surplus book depository will reveal whole rooms filled with such efforts, with fresh ones constantly on their way from the bindery, their plain black and forest green covers embossed with the gold-lettered titles, *Angelic Movements: The Dawson at a Glance* or, though it might seem shameless, *Ode to a Dawson*. So while there is a great quantity of literature readily available on this animalculum (a great deal more than can be found on any other creature in this book), almost none of it could be considered properly useful.

Perhaps the only relevant work on the subject was written in 1926 by a Dr. Aplsey Conway, entitled, simply, *The Dawson Observed*. Conway focuses not on the dawson itself, but on this phenomenon of affection (and subsequent frustration) that it tends to elicit in those who study it. His book is, therefore, predominantly a work of psychology and much of Conway's evidence is—here we must truly express our regret—literary. However, since it is our intention to help introduce you to this creature, it might also serve to prepare you for what will certainly be your own range of emotions once you have been introduced. Because surely—though you have not yet seen a dawson—your cheeks have already grown flushed over our description. Surely, you are already nervous and agitated over the prospect of something which has proven to be somewhat of a universal temptation.

Conway's work hinges significantly on a point mentioned briefly above. That is: "All animalcula are so small that, though they are all around us, it is as if they exist on a different plane than our own, one impossibly distant," etc., etc. It is this fact, according to Conway, that inevitably causes an observer's affection for the dawson to develop into the profoundest anxiety. In way of an explanation, Conway launches into a lengthy and also somewhat unlikely discussion of Ancient Roman poetry:

> Ultimately, it is not the knowledge that his desires are perverse that causes the observer any consternation. Rather, it is due to the paradox that presents itself when one considers that the observer is exceedingly close to his beloved, has only to extend his hand a matter of inches in order to caress it. However, due to the discrepancy in their size, the two are separated by an infinite distance.
>
> One is reminded of the classical poetic convention of the paraclausithyron, a popular motif in Roman love elegies of the Augustan period, in which a lover, *amator exclusus*, is separated from his beloved by a door. The works of Catullus, Horace, Ovid, and Tibullus contain several poems of lovers pounding on doors, weeping at them, pleading and reasoning with the doors themselves, threatening to knock them to smithereens.
>
> However, just as it is with the observer and his dawson, the barrier between the lover and the beloved in a paraclausithyron is not strictly a physical one. The nature of a door separating lovers is more complicated than simply its value as a physical presence. Doors are ruled by individuals, who are themselves ruled by ideas. Though the lover's physical proximity to the object of his desire is

close, is precisely the mere width of a door, an idea has created an enormous breach between him and his beloved. And so, by focusing his frustration on the door itself, the lover is essentially recognizing that, because of the hungers resulting from his affection, his proximity to the object of his desire is no longer ruled by physical space.

So while an observer is not kept apart from the dawson by any physical barrier and is, in fact, as close to the object of his affection as any lover could wish, nevertheless, like the *amator exclusus*, the observer is deprived of the realization of his love by what he recognizes as an abstraction. For the observer caught in the dawson's spell, there develops a terrific frustration at the belief that a perfectly plausible love is being obstructed by an invisible matrix of senseless and petty *ideas*. This belief is in turn nurtured by the observer's close-and-yet-so-far relationship to the dawson, which, like the *amator exclusus*, has helped him to unhinge his ideas regarding physical space.

In order to further understand the mania that follows this sense of non-physical exclusion, one is assisted greatly by a further reading of the poet Ovid. Because even though the physical presence of the door in a paraclausithyron is marginal compared to what that door represents, one is still forced to admit that there is a physical barrier between the poet and his beloved. No matter what abstractions may keep the door in a paraclausithyron fixed shut, because the door remains a physical obstruction in at least one sense, it is still possible to imagine the lover finally breaking through that door, destroying it to the half-fear and excitement of his beloved, tearing her tunic in his haste, tussling her hair, whimpering like a small boy as he gently bites her lips. And so, the parallel between the *amator exclusus* and the dawson's observer can only be taken so far.

That would be the end of it, except that in Ovid's *Metamorphoses*, the poet does something incredible. He writes a paraclausithyron, but takes away the door: Picture a young man, exceptionally handsome. Tired from a day of hunting, he seeks refuge from the summer sun in the shade of a small cluster of trees. There, he finds a lush carpet of grass surrounding a small pond. Thirsty, he leans over it to drink. And just like that, Narcissus is transfixed. The lips of his beloved beg for a kiss, but, when he leans forward, he finds nothing. He attempts to embrace his beloved, but his arms only disperse the image of his goal into a chaos of rippling water. In his frustration, Narcissus cries out, "Has anyone loved more cruelly?" He suffers all the more, because he and his lover are not divided by an immense ocean, roads, mountains, or walls with sealed gates. "We are kept apart," he mourns, "by a mere bit of water . . . the thinnest barrier obstructs our loving embraces."

In this story, one begins to see more clearly the nature of what separates the observer from the dawson. It is the same thin, watery membrane that separates fact from illusion. It is that border between the real and the imagined world, which manages to create such a paradox of distance. The observer is close to the dawson; Narcissus is, by the very act of being alive, as close to Narcissus as one could ever become, but, because of that slender partition between the real and the unreal, great seas of loneliness will open up between the lover and the loved.

As you can see, Conway writes on the subject with a great deal of passion. His arguments, though often frenetic and arbitrary, succeed terrifically in detailing the troubled and jumbled mindset of any individual who might find himself falling in love with a very tiny creature. It is uncertain whether or not Conway had any personal experience in observing the dawson, but the complexity of his insight seems to suggest that he did. Shortly after the publication of his book, he engaged in a national lecture tour regarding the possibilities of human miniaturization before dying of a self-inflicted gunshot wound in a parking lot just outside Duluth.

Naturally, none of this is to suggest that it is impossible to observe the dawson extensively, while still going on to lead a perfectly happy life. Many a time has a young scientist peered down at a dawson through a microscope and many a time has a cooler head prevailed. However, the warning is still valid. And though it is not impossible to live a satisfied life while pursuing knowledge of the dawson, it is more difficult. Even we, your authors—having deliberately taken a cursory approach to studying the dawson, keeping to still photographs and written reports, glancing at a live dawson perhaps only a half dozen times in our distinguished careers—even we can find ourselves, in our quieter moments, drifting into a kind of reverie over this remarkable creature, only to be startled back to the present by a concerned spouse placing a hand on our shoulder. Even we, at times, are haunted in the night by half-visions of dawsons moving gracefully in the air, in the darkness above our beds. And so, though we would encourage you to study the dawson as carefully as you wish, if you value your happiness, we suggest that you restrict yourself to the following: Look briefly, and then—if you can—look away.

— ELDRIT —

When observed, the eldrit changes. Once its characteristics and tendencies are documented, it adopts new characteristics, new tendencies. A researcher observes that the eldrit propels itself by means of long, translucent flagella. The researcher writes:

> *Flagella, translucent,*
> *means of locomotion*

But as soon as he returns his attention to the eldrit, he finds that it now propels itself by means of a slight undulation of its belly. The flagella, now bright orange, are being used to expel waste. The researcher makes a note of this and then finds that the eldrit in question is suddenly stationary. Its flagella have disappeared altogether.

It will most likely be surprising to you that the scientific community has no idea how the eldrit is able to accomplish such dramatic mutations. However, keep in mind that the mechanics of an ant walking along the vein of a leaf is enough to make all the technological advancements of the last three centuries look like the output of an eighth grade wood shop: wobbling tables, misspelled signs, precarious rocking horses unevenly stained. Human achievement and understanding are constantly being dwarfed by the complexity of the natural world.

So how do scientists address this question of the eldrit's ability to alter itself? We step around it, nodding politely as we pass. As a scientist, it is often the only acceptable method to ignore an impossible question, which, if history serves, will most likely be answered accidentally by someone setting out to answer something else.

Rather, most research regarding the eldrit is concerned not with how it changes itself, but why. Because if one accepts the assertion that the first priority of all living organisms is self-preservation, then one must conclude that the eldrit's very existence serves as an argument that there is something caustic in being identified, in having the boundaries of one's physical and behavioral makeup established.

In fact, this seems almost intuitive. Once the characteristics of a creature are fixed, it is given a role to fill as a result of those characteristics. Through the act of being itself, either a creature becomes the one forced to attach itself as a parasite to a lower intestine, where it will depend on that organ for the most foul sustenance imaginable, or else it becomes the one whose lower intestine is thus infested. Certainly, neither position could be said to inspire envy. But because each creature allows itself to be itself, both positions are unavoidable.

The evolutionary adaptations that creatures undergo in order to alleviate their circumstances are—at best—only half-solutions and—at worst—further provocations of hardship. The haunch muscles that aid the antelope in its flight from predators are also an excellent source of protein. The bear's massive strength betrays its equally massive capacity to starve to death.

But while other creatures change themselves in response to the environmental pressures that affect their various roles, the eldrit seems to change in order to shun the notion that it has a role to fill in the first place. Furthermore, the eldrit does not depend on a Punnett square in order to carry out these changes. Instead, it changes instantly. So in the exact moment that one creature is just beginning to realize, after hundreds of thousands of years of genetic alterations, that an elongated snout is not nearly as useful as perhaps its ancestors had supposed, the eldrit is growing two dozen snouts per minute, stretching them out farther and farther. Just as quickly, the eldrit allows its snouts to fall off and desiccate.

Though before we regard the eldrit's position as being totally advantageous, it should also be mentioned that, on account of its compulsive tendency to change, the eldrit misses out on one of the most pleasing aspects of being a creature, which is, simply put, *being* a creature.

Among all living things, there is a certain joy in being recognizable as oneself. Even those of us whose bodies are a constant source of apprehension and awkwardness take comfort in seeing our faces in the mirror at the end of the day. As young scientists, you are all no doubt very unattractive. Yet, there is something reassuring in knowing that you have taken a shape, however unfortunate. It is something that is utterly yours, and no matter how miserable you might look while standing in your underwear or how ill at ease you might be in a bathing suit, when you are being honest with yourself, you enjoy your shape; you take solace in it. Think: When people feel dejected and forlorn, they often hold their own heads in their hands. Why do they do this, if not to take consolation in the fact that they have a definite form, that they are in the possession of something entirely their own?

This notion that all creatures possess inalienable qualities, which represent an incorruptible sense of self, exists on an evolutionary scale as well. Just look at the transformation of dinosaurs into birds. The dinosaur might not mind diminishing in size or growing wings, but to stop laying eggs? To begin shaping its skeleton differently or its heart? To give up the beautifully vacant eyes of a reptile? The savage waggle of its neck? Unthinkable. That is why researchers are now attempting to determine if, in all the eldrit's responses to the observations directed at it, there are any qualities that refuse to change and are quintessentially itself.

A common approach is to have a live video feed of an eldrit's magnified image broadcast onto a large monitor where it is then viewed by a room filled with observers, all of whom stare intently at the image and direct as many observations at it as possible. The manic and prolonged ripple of changes that this exercise produces in the eldrit is recorded for posterity and then viewed repeatedly by researchers attempting to establish some sort of constant in the eldrit. The hope is that if a great enough number of observations is directed at a single eldrit for a long enough period of time, the creature will eventually become overwhelmed and begin to falter, inadvertently revealing its secret consistencies.

No such breakthrough has occurred.

As the number of observations directed at an eldrit increase, so does the eldrit's ambiguity. On a monitor in an observation room, an eldrit takes on a series of indescribable shapes, splits itself in two, reabsorbs itself, becomes bright pink. It trembles slightly and then explodes. It reassembles itself. Explodes. Reassembles itself. Explodes.

One must admit that even the meekest creature ends up seeming bold in comparison. Consider the gazelle. There is an unmistakable bravery in its implicit admission that, through being a gazelle, it is a gazelle. And even though one can hardly look at its long, delicate neck without immediately thinking of the powerful jaws that will inevitably snap it in two, the gazelle does not shirk its post. It manages to take responsibility for what it is, while the eldrit can only change unconditionally, a slave to its wild, untouchable freedom.

* * *

— KESSEL —

The lifespan of an average kessel is four one-hundred-millionths of a second. To put this figure into perspective: If you were to fire a .30 caliber rifle at an opposing target fifty feet away, 462,963 generations of kessel would pass by the time the bullet reached the target. If you were to hold a handkerchief six inches from your nose and sneeze into it, 8,522,727 generations of kessel would pass in the time it took for the mucus to reach the handkerchief. But numbers do little to convey the extreme brevity of a kessel's life. Rather, imagine a newborn infant flashing from its mother's womb like a lightning bolt and arriving in the doctor's arms as a full-grown skeleton already crumbling to dust.

Naturally, observing the kessel is rather difficult. Its death follows its birth so closely that it is impossible to distinguish one process from the other. In fact, the three major acts of a living creature (birth, procreation, and death) are so compressed in time that the kessel seems to accomplish all three by means of a single exertion.

Even the experienced observer, aided by recent technological developments in high-speed photography, will find it impossible to differentiate the characteristics of a dying kessel from one that's just been born or a sexually mature kessel from one not yet fully developed, because it is all these things at once. In the kessel, each stage of life informs the other simultaneously.

Though strange, this quality of simultaneity should not

be considered altogether remote from human experience. Who has not occasionally seen death as a weary nod toward birth and vice versa? Who has not occasionally recognized the link between sex and death? Young lovers, as they embrace, are often already able to sense the coming of a private apocalypse in the thumping of their lovers' hearts. Ailing men and women, as they lie on their deathbeds, are often said to feel as if they are being slowly undressed, as if they are expecting a release, which, as it first approaches, is at once frightening, painful, and secretly exhilarating.

Throughout the ages, human beings have viewed the transition from birth to sexual maturity to death as a necessary progression. The notion that these things are distinct from one another, that they form a grand narrative, is a social construction that many people have internalized as an indisputable fact. So it is understandable that the existence of the kessel happens to make many people uncomfortable. What kind of parents would want to be told that their newborn child is an aspect of death? Or, worse, that their child has sexual implications beyond the gentle copulation that produced it?

The manner in which the kessel's existence informs our own can be incredibly disheartening. Its cells begin to form and break down at the same time, and so, when successfully recorded and played back on video streams slowed to infinitesimal proportions, these cells produce a tesseractic movement, folding down into themselves continuously without altering their shape. This motion would be hypnotic if it weren't so brief. Even with the video slowed, the cells disappear in an instant. This sight is, in a word, depressing. It makes us—who are fond of saying to one another under various circumstances that life is, in fact, too short—seem like the worst sort of gluttons.

On the other hand, the smallness and brevity of a kessel's existence begin to remind one of how small and brief our existence is on a universal scale. Stars die. Galaxies collide. And everything in the universe that is human, the sum of all our ambitions, histories, fears, achievements, and failures, exists on the head of a needle.

In consideration of the kessel, human nature seems to be open to two conflicting criticisms. The first is that we see our average lifespan as being insufficient, despite the fact that the time afforded to a stillborn seems decadent when compared to the life of a kessel, and despite the fact that we still find time enough to be bored and to wish for time to move faster. While the second criticism is that we see our average lifespan as sufficient and that the actions contained therein are significant. We flatter ourselves with the assumption that anything of importance can be accomplished in our seventy to eighty years when the earth has been around for billions of years and has been known to change dominant species as if they were hats. Our pity for the kessel is revealed as naive in that, if you judge a kessel's existence by the amount of time that elapses in the human world and judge a human's existence by the amount of time that elapses in the universe, then we disappear from our surroundings even faster than the kessel disappears from its own.

This is particularly disconcerting because, though at odds,

both arguments seem valid. And so, along with the already grim content of these criticisms, comes the hurtful reminder that human beings are riddled with absurdities and contradictions even with respect to something as simple as our faults.

The whole issue of the kessel as it relates to our existence is ultimately filled with so much unmitigated glumness that many consider it to be an inappropriate topic for polite conversation. Details regarding the kessel are among the type of coldhearted facts that are inevitably mentioned at parties by angry young men who wish to impress upon anyone having more fun than themselves that the world is, in fact, little more than a brutal joke. Most researchers who specialize in the kessel end up adopting this air of arrogance and scorn. They are typically unkempt, wild-looking. Their faces are ravaged by distrust, and they are always ready with a discouraging remark.

It makes sense that scientists who watch that sad footage again and again—the kessel fluttering briefly and then vanishing—would eventually give in to despair. Further, it makes sense that those who are confronted on a daily basis by those criticisms of our nature mentioned above would eventually begin to despise our nature. But based on their studies of the kessel, these people are ready to conclude that everything we hold dear is futile and amounts to nothing. However, the fact remains that such a view of the kessel and of human nature is incomplete.

For example, the kessel mates for life. At first, this might seem unimpressive, owing to the fact that life for a kessel is a brisk four one-hundred-millionths of a second. But because it is sexually mature even before it is born, the average kessel spends a greater percentage of its lifetime with its mate than any other creature on earth, a relationship which is strictly monogamous and most resembles our understanding of romantic love.

Granted, some researchers argue that it maintains one mate because it simply does not have the time to take on another. Dr. Richard Koch—unkempt and wild-looking, Koch is a preeminent figure among the kessel specialists mentioned briefly above—is a strong proponent of this theory. In a recent study, Koch examined the mating practices of the kessel, focusing on the kessel's speed and urgency in an attempt to establish its promiscuity.

But Koch's own study contains evidence to the contrary. Buried in indexes and supplemental figures are instances of kessels who chose somewhat older mates, outlived them, and then spent the rest of their short lives in mourning. In fact, this is rather common. A kessel that is two one-hundred-billionths of a second old might select a mate that is one one-hundred-millionths of a second old. When the latter dies, the former does not seek a replacement but spends the rest of its life in solitude. There are also instances of kessels which, seeking an ideal mate, have waited in absolute celibacy a staggering three one-hundred-millionths of a second.

These instances of self-imposed isolation are remarkable, especially when one considers the fact that the kessel tends to crave desperately the company of its own kind. Experiments have been conducted in which a single specimen has been separated from a larger group by a tenth of a millimeter. These experiments show that the lone kessel will spend its entire life moving back toward its fellows despite the fact that a tenth of a millimeter—for a creature which, in addition to being so small and short-lived, is not particularly fast—is like the distance between two stars. In some primal fashion, the kessel must understand that it is an impossible distance. And yet, it persists.

So, yes, it's true: the universe is massive, whereas we are small and quickly fading. But things are never as hopeless as people like Koch would have you believe. There are still opportunities for happiness for those willing to accept existence for what it is. Even a creature like the kessel seems to understand the transformative capabilities of something as simple as affection. It fixates on companionship in what seems like deliberate ignorance of the fact that it is surrounded by larger and larger worlds. When it finally finds its mate, the kessel exhausts its life in that purest intimacy, without a care, as its one moment goes rushing past.

— MELITE —

Small, spore-like creatures, melites are born in pairs. Each melite is initially attached to its sibling by a thin tendril of tissue. Once born, they are lifted up on the first light breeze, which causes that delicate tendril to strain and then snap. Separated, the two are carried off on diverging winds. As soon as it is severed from its sibling, a melite begins to writhe and spasm, attempting to wriggle back toward its birth-mate. These spasms cause its body to be pulled taut against the wind, making it sail out even more dramatically in long arcs away from its sibling. It spends its entire life like this, frantically convulsing in midair in an effort to return to its ideal state, and, in doing so, casting itself farther and farther out.

— BARTLETT —

Like so many discoveries that influence our understanding of the world, our knowledge of the bartlett is based primarily on conjecture. It is neither visible to the naked eye nor visible under any degree of magnification currently available to us. It leaves no trace of itself in its environment. It is neither beneficial nor detrimental to surrounding creatures, who react to its presence not at all. First documented by Richard Bartlett in 1890, it was discovered when, in the middle of an experiment, Bartlett's assistant inadvertently replaced a prepared specimen dish with a fresh one. Bartlett recognized the incredible nature of his discovery almost immediately. The bartlett requires no resources and expels no waste. In the living world, with its savage, intricate web of infinite species infinitely interconnected, the bartlett seems somehow set apart—existing entirely on its own terms. It has no characteristics known to us, except that, practically speaking, it has none. Many consider the bartlett to be exceptionally rare while others suspect that it might be the most plentiful creature on earth. There is some controversy among certain academic factions who claim that the bartlett cannot rightly be considered a creature. Their argument being that—to their thinking—its existence cannot be tested. This, of course, could not be further from the truth. If one desires to test for the presence of a bartlett, all that has to be done is to check for the presence of any characteristic exhibited by any creature on earth. If none is found, well, there is your bartlett.

Certainly, some of you may ask: Even if it can be considered a creature, what is the value of studying it? If it cannot be observed, if it is seemingly without cause or effect, then what could possibly be learned from it? It is an astute question, to be sure. However, you might as well ask yourself why you desire to be a scientist at all. You might as well ask yourself why you are holding this book, why you are only pretending to have a genuine interest in the nature of the world and, in doing so, wasting everyone's time. Because even if a creature does nothing, creates nothing, destroys nothing, requires nothing, to a true scientist its existence will matter. To be a person of science, one must understand that even if we were to grasp flawlessly all the causes and effects of the world, all its various functions, we would never have a full view of it if we did not take into account that there are creatures that do nothing, that seem neither the impetus nor the result of anything. So, if the study of such a creature displeases you, maybe it is for the best that you put this book down. As you do so, we ask that you be careful of the binding, so that this volume might survive long enough to prove useful to those more sincere in their pursuits.

This admonishment having been offered, it should be mentioned—for those of you who continue to read—that knowledge of the bartlett is predominately useless for a young scientist such as yourself. Understanding the principles of this creature will be of no real advantage to you as a student, and so no further information concerning it will be given. While the ideal curiosity of the true scientist was mentioned above, it is actually rather doubtful that any of you will continue on in this field long enough or with enough vigor, determination, or brilliance for your philosophical stance on the purpose of observation to be of any consequence to anyone. Though you should keep in mind that your understanding of the bartlett can still function as a strong and revealing personal state-ment. Not as a scientist, but as an individual. Remember that, while your thoughts may never be of importance to others, your potency as an individual is that your mind still has the ability to change the assumed nature of the world in which those thoughts are formed. And one must be certain that there is a difference between living in a world in which nothing is simply nothing and in which nothing is a bartlett. The differ-ence may seem slight, but civilizations have faded over lesser nuance. In fact, that is just the point. When a civilization fades, how does it fade? Does it collapse into nothing? Or do all those people and buildings and great works dissolve into a cloud of bartletts? For that matter, what happens to your loved ones when they die? Do they disappear? Or is their death a final metamorphosis and dispersion into these small creatures that swirl around us everywhere, full of secrets that are locked tight and silenced by the nature of their void characteristic? Does the world in which you live eventually terminate into a murky sea of nothing? Or does it happily mix itself with these creatures that are full of great and complex meaning, which, though inaccessible, would still exist, if you would only acknowledge it?

— BASTROM —

It was not long after its discovery that the commercial implications of the bastrom became apparent. Here we are not referring to the discovery of its existence but of its culinary potential, which was established by an amateur biologist named Alexander Beltley—a man who occupies a strange place in scientific history because he was never able to explain how or why his specimen dish made its way into his mouth on that fateful day of August 17, 1966. Whatever Beltley's motivations were in consuming a tablespoon of live, agitated bastrom, one can be certain that his actions have left an indelible mark on the world.

In short, the bastrom is delicious.

To this day, in addition to the salt and pepper shakers on our kitchen tables, there is a third shaker. As children you were no doubt taught two holes for pepper, three for salt, and four for bastrom. The discrepancy in the number of holes at the mouth of the shaker has always been a useful precaution in the telling apart of salt and pepper, but in the case of bastrom it is for the most part unnecessary. In order to determine which is filled with bastrom, one only has to look for the shaker that incessantly trembles and hops about the table, the shaker with a distinctly wider base meant to prevent it from toppling itself, the shaker that is fastened to the table by means of a short, beaded chain like a pen at a bank counter.

Though small, bastrom are capable of communal spasms which are a fear-response to their being kept in such a confined space. It is a peculiarity of this creature that the more frightened or in pain it is, the better it tastes. That is why, when a shaker of bastrom whips itself around wildly, chipping plates and making a racket, this nuisance is not only tolerated but encouraged.

When frightened, the bastrom releases a chemical compound called diebulkide, a mildly acidic substance which is meant to irritate the eyes of the klempate, the bastrom's chief predator prior to 1966. This compound reacts pleasantly on the human tongue, so this adaptation, which was meant to protect the bastrom from one predator, has in turn made it vulnerable to another.

The bastrom can only be eaten alive, as, logically, a dead creature cannot be frightened. Knowledgeable eaters will place a small cube of potato in their bastrom shakers, as providing the creatures with sustenance will allow them to survive far longer than without. A true gourmand might also keep a small box of matches next to the shaker, the idea being to wave a lit match over the bodies of the bastrom once they have been shaken out onto a particular dish, so that the pain and resulting anxiety created by the flame will increase the amount of diebulkide that those bastrom release.

Though being crammed into the confines of a shaker will cause enough discomfort to make bastrom flavorful, many prefer this tactic of deliberately increasing the level of anxiety in their bastrom in order to achieve the most flavor possible. In addition to the flame technique, some prefer to use a pair of cymbals while they eat, stopping every so often to make huge, crashing sounds over their plates. Others simply prefer to lean in close and speak to their plates in a deliberately cruel tone of voice.

But what has been learned over time is that the acidic properties of diebulkide will inevitably wear out a person's taste buds. So these individuals who go to extra lengths to enjoy the taste of the bastrom's fear are also the quickest to render themselves insensitive to it. These people are forced to crash the cymbals over their plates with such force that the noise is unbearable even to themselves. Rather than waving the lit match lightly over their food, these people press the flame down into it until it turns black, until whatever hint of diebulkide that registers on their tongues is overwhelmed by the taste of ash. Instead of only speaking cruelly to their food, they scream. They pound on the table with their fists. They adopt an attitude of genuine hatred toward the bastrom. When they are alone, they attempt to dream up new acts of violence which they hope will help bring back some sensation to that one part of themselves that has grown so hard of feeling.

— PRINCIPLES OF OBSERVATION —

In the same way that it is difficult to think of a distant planet as being an actual place—as real as the ground beneath your feet—it is often difficult to think of most animalcula as being actual creatures. Like a planet viewed through a telescope, one tends to recognize an animalculum viewed through a microscope not as a thing, but as an image of a thing. Though both instruments manipulate reality in only the most rudimentary fashion, bringing objects closer or making them larger, we still understand that what we are seeing is a deception. Our minds take in what is seen by means of those instruments with the same reflexive disbelief with which we have learned to greet the computer-generated monsters in the summer blockbuster, the map of Texas behind the meteorologist, the digitally altered photograph in a magazine of JFK drinking a Pepsi.

At this point in history, a healthy sense of skepticism with respect to images is increasingly necessary. Otherwise, every single soap commercial would break our hearts. Every advertisement featuring a beautiful woman lying on a white-sanded beach in the ecstasy of whatever product would corrupt us not only with a desire for that product but also with the belief that our life is pale and undesirable, something that needs desperately to be fixed. And so we lean on our skepticism for balance. We roll our eyes at that woman on the beach. We hold at arm's length all the deliberately phony images of the everyday, the pervasiveness of which so harasses us that we are no longer able to differentiate false images from true ones.

Likewise, when students first observe the characteristics of an animalculum through a microscope, it is as if they are only taking note of the ridiculous assurances in yet another commercial or parsing a news broadcast for its biases and inconsistencies. Even those few students who do feel a connection with their subject [SEE DAWSON] will readily admit to the limitations and frustrations that are involved in dedicating oneself to what is, for all practical purposes, little more than a moving picture.

However, before you allow this skepticism to taint your research, keep in mind that your own vision manipulates reality more than any microscope ever could. Far less distortion takes place between the objective lens and eyepiece of a microscope than takes place in your own mind when you stare at your feet in the bath. This is by no means an exaggeration: Your mind interprets the retinal input of your feet soaking in the tub by means of a complex system of inference, using its accumulated knowledge of how far away from your eyes your feet tend to be, of where the source of light in your bathroom tends to come from, of how light tends to move through soapy water. In short, your mind cross-checks all the combinations that could create this retinal input against the input's given context, so that what you experience as the image of your own feet has less to do with the reality of your feet at that moment than it does with your brain's efforts to provide you with an image that makes sense.

So if the era in which you live has made you skeptical with respect to manipulated images, then you must accept that this skepticism applies to the visual world as a whole, and that there is no real difference between a computer-animated dinosaur and your own hand held out in front of your face.

After embracing this, you have two options: 1.) You can reject everything, and regard the world as a baseless fiction, or 2.) You can take the information that your senses give you, albeit incomplete and interpretive, and attempt to derive from it rules and principles. You can accept the fact that science is an operation of faith, and that in order to participate in it you must first reject the fear that a false image could make you foolish.

— HALIFITE —

Before the discovery of the halifite, the scientific community was in agreement that an emotion was a response to a state of being. In the same way that the concept of time is used to keep track of objects moving through space, it was believed that the purpose of emotion was to help individuals keep track of themselves as they moved from one state of being to another. Just as it is easier to delineate one's physical existence by means of the artificial units of hours, minutes, and seconds— quantities which are significant only because they have been widely agreed upon—our prehalifite understanding of emotion maintained that quantities such as happiness and sadness were likewise only artificial, convenient points of reference.

This view of emotion as a mechanical response to the progress of our fortunes seems immediately naive to those of us who experience emotions on a daily basis. Contemporary readers, such as yourselves, will have difficulty understanding how the prehalifite view was ever taken seriously. However, before you condemn those who came before you for their ignorance, keep in mind that without the insights afforded to us by the halifite, the prehalifite view would still be unassailable fact.

The halifite tends to be found on the bodies of large mammals. Subsisting on dead skin cells, it goes generally unnoticed. It is oval in shape with a pale blue outer cuticle. It most resembles and is often mistaken for an exceptionally small variety of dust mite. However, in addition to its size, the halifite is distinguished by its uncanny ability to emote.

One does not have to observe a halifite for long before it begins to exhibit behavior that is altogether singular and which, to the uninitiated, might seem delightful. A halifite stands upright on the tip of an eyelash while happily doing a sort of soft-shoe routine. Another halifite is on its knees, beating its chest and pulling melodramatically at its antennae. These exhibitions of—there can be no question—emotion tend to be entertaining to lay observers in the same perverse and universal way that it is often considered funny to see a farm animal dressed in women's clothing or a dog smoking a pipe. Halifitic expressions of emotion contain elements of the same madcap anthropomorphism which is the ruling principle of Saturday morning cartoons and children's books. For this reason, much like the ridiculous-looking frilled-neck lizard and the overtly adorable panda cub, images of halifite have become a staple for the covers of elementary school science textbooks in their belabored attempts to convince children that science can be fun.

But presenting the halifite's behavior to students in this way drastically undermines its importance. It is also extremely disrespectful to the inner experience of such a sensitive creature. Not pictured on the cover of those textbooks are all the halifite that, overwhelmed by their own emotional experience, have hanged themselves from a host's earlobe or deliberately bashed their own heads open on a patch of dry skin.

When studying the halifite, keep in mind that there is no difference between its joys and your joys, between its sorrows and your sorrows. If you perceive a difference, what is it? That the halifite is small? That it does not have language or a higher intellect? Don't be a snob. Feeling is feeling. Also, remember that it is only on account of the halifite's inner experience that we are beginning to better understand our own.

In this respect, the halifite initially seems to confirm the idea that emotion is a direct response to a state of being. That is, the halifite seems to use its emotions as a way of processing external stimuli in a way that adheres to common sense. Pleasant stimuli correspond to happiness, unpleasant stimuli to sadness.

Example: An adult, female halifite returns to her nest to find that her eggs have been destroyed by a competitor. The halifite probes the ruined eggs with her antennae and shows obvious signs of mourning.

However, when the observer increases the level of magnification, the emotion exhibited by the halifite in question suddenly changes. In response to the demise of her eggs, the halifite is now expressing a guarded sense of relief, as if she has been freed from a tremendous burden. When the level of magnification is increased again, the halifite is consumed with guilt. As the magnification is increased again, the halifite is convulsing in a kind of laughter, which is unmistakably at her own expense. As the magnification is increased again, the halifite is bowing her head toward the destroyed eggs in the grips of some bizarre and reverent joy. As the magnification is increased yet again, the halifite's expression is frozen in a mask of grotesque horror.

With every incremental adjustment to the level of magnification, the observer will discover a new, discernable emotion in the halifite. The emotion being expressed at the lowest level of magnification—in this case, mourning—is actually a composite of all the emotions being expressed at the greater levels

of magnification. Far from being a pure, clear-cut phenomenon, the halifite shows us that a single observable emotion
is really only the most obvious facet of the complex interplay
among all possible emotions.

On account of this insight, many inner events which would
have been regarded as insane under the prehalifite view are
now understood to be perfectly natural. In an unexpected
moment, the widow laughs into the casket. The businessman
grieves over his profits. The assassin swoons for the king. Our
emotions never wholly reflect our state of being because we
are experiencing every possible emotion at all times, just in
varying proportions. So it is when we are sad that our happiness most surprises us. It is when we are pleased that our sadness most perplexes us. It is when we are prepared to slit the
king's throat that our love for him is the most startling.

But if emotion is not a direct response to our state of
being, then what function does it serve? This question that
the prehalifite view perceived as being so crucial is, of course,
ridiculous. It neglects the fact that the universe is a hairy, tan-
gled mess filled with purposeless digressions, of which our
entire emotional framework is most likely just one among
the uncountable. At any rate, be wary of those who would
attempt to judge things solely by their function. The world is
not an implement.

We must begin to approach the idea that, perhaps, emotion exists for emotion's sake, and that what makes our inner
events so intense and manifestly difficult to understand is
that the end toward which all emotion is moving is unknown

even to its own components. And if this uncertainty troubles you or leaves you feeling depressed, then examine your feelings carefully and take note of the fact that you are also thrilled by it.

— KIRKLIN —

All kirklin currently occupy a space no larger than an acorn. This arrangement should be impossible, as there are currently ninety-five trillion kirklin in existence, and each is roughly the size of a grain of rice. The compression of their entire species into such a small space is an incredible feat, and, in terms of understanding it, the scientific community is at a loss.

In 1988, a physicist at Yale by the name of Dr. Josephine Klemp attempted to duplicate the kirklin's compression using 200,000 popsicle sticks in a pressurized chamber. The resulting explosion killed the thirty-eight graduate students who had been working under Klemp and destroyed the better part of Yale's historic Abbot Building where the study was located.

Klemp was not in the lab when the explosion occurred and went on to publish a somewhat controversial paper based on the data she collected regarding the force with which the popsicle sticks had blown through the skulls of her former assistants. While many found the paper to be in poor taste, the fact is that by extrapolating that data and applying it to the kirklin, Klemp was the first to raise the question of the potential force that might be implied by the kirklin's compression. Klemp pointed out that because the level of compression achieved in her study was only a fraction of that which exists within the kirklin population cluster, the explosion that occurred in her study was only a fraction of what would result if the cluster were to suffer a similar instability. In short, Klemp raised the fear that a kirklinic explosion would cause our entire planet to share a fate similar to that of Yale's Abbot Building.

However, over the years, many experts have argued against this view. Prominent physicist Dr. Quentin Butler describes Klemp's explosion theory as foolishness. According to Butler, the notion that Klemp's compression of popsicle sticks is any way analogous to the current state of the kirklin is unfounded. Butler contends that given the extreme density of the kirklin cluster, the creatures are far more likely to implode, creating a giant black hole that would consume our solar system and go on to gnaw away at the surrounding universe.

Others maintain that Butler's view is no more realistic than Klemp's. Dr. Alfonzo Delgado, former director of the Conklin Institute, derides both views as pseudoscientific. He claims it is far more likely that instability in the kirklin cluster would spark a chain reaction in which the kirklin would cause everything that came in contact with it to become similarly compressed. Dr. Marie Cabot-Berger, at the Trevor Laboratories, describes a theory in which the kirklin might corrupt the vacuum of space, causing the entire universe to disappear at the speed of light.

While opinion varies greatly as to how it would happen, all experts seem to be unanimous in the assumption that the kirklin is on the brink of ending the world. The popular press has seized on this anxiety, and every two weeks there is a new theory being put forth in which the kirklin will destroy life as we know it. And while some theories are more difficult to disprove than others, it is important to remember in each case that because what is being feared is without precedent, there can ultimately be no real evidence to support it. What is being expressed in these conjectures is simply the natural human fear of catastrophe, the perennial concern that the sky will fall, that the earth will open up, that all the aspects of the universe that we cannot control will finally come to bear. These fears are ancient, and science has simply put new words to them, given them a new, compressed shape.

— KAYLITE —

For every kaylite that dies, roughly four trillion new kaylite are born. Because they are so small, this massive population growth is at the moment unnoticeable. A cluster of kaylite sits throbbing on the sidewalk and is mistaken by passersby for a small rust-colored stone. Two hundred trillion kaylite converge on a windowpane and are mistaken for a dirty fingerprint. But because their number is growing exponentially, within ten years that window will go dark and then crack. Our great-grandchildren will stand around that rust-colored stone which will suddenly be the size of a barn. They will form a bucket brigade, dousing it with boric acid in an attempt to diminish that unsightly, steadily increasing mass. As the centuries progress, whole islands of kaylite will rise up out of the ocean. Old mountain ranges will be dwarfed by their new, trembling counterparts. Regarding these bizarre changes in the landscape, our descendants will no doubt think back in wonder on the days when these seemingly boundless growths were mistaken for pebbles, when they could have been ground out beneath a boot heel without a second thought.

— LASAR —

Bloodshed between species is constant and essential. Without it, predators would starve for want of food, and prey would collapse under the weight of their ever-expanding populations. However, violence within a single species is comparatively rare. When it occurs, it is typically restrained and ritualized. For instance, a rattlesnake does not make use of its deadly poison when fighting another rattlesnake. Instead, it will wrestle with its opponent in a predetermined ceremony, in which each snake harmlessly attempts to pin the other to the ground.

So while rattlesnakes will not hesitate to kill an unsuspecting child or a curious dog, when it comes to one rattlesnake pitted against another, the two will typically choose to settle the thing like gentlemen. The same is true when two elk deliberately clap antlers or when two elephants lock tusks or when an African saplid empties its ink pouch onto a rock adjacent to a competing saplid's egg mound.

Unrestrained conflict between animals of the same species is not unheard of, but, through the logic of natural selection, it is far from being the rule. In addition to the fact that it is a costly expenditure of energy, the risk of being seriously injured is as real for the attacker as it is for the animal being attacked. If such conflict can be avoided, most creatures do just that.

However, a notable exception to this is the lasar. A stout, round little creature, it will attempt to kill any other lasar it comes into contact with by ramming into it repeatedly. Since the other lasar will conduct itself in the exact same way, the probability of any lasar surviving one of these contests is roughly the same as a coin toss. Existence, for a lasar, is little more than a succession of purposeless murders ending inevitably in its own.

The ritualized fighting of other creatures is typically attached to disputes over territory, resources, and sexual dominance, whereas the all-out conflict that exists between lasar is attached to none of these. Therefore, the lasar is thought to be the only creature on earth other than man capable of governing itself by means of an ideology—by which is simply meant that its behavior has somehow been elevated above common sense.

There is no way to determine the content of the lasar's ideology, as ideologies, in general, have no content. They are only indications of a failure to incorporate oneself into the natural world. That the lasar insists on killing other lasar is merely an example of this kind of failure. Unsurprisingly, it is an endangered species. This is seemingly of its own accord, and the fact that there might one day be no more lasars to speak of seems less the result of its shortsightedness than of whatever vague promise it perceives in its own vicious and unstoppable cruelty.

— PAGLUM —

The paglum is compelled to imitate whatever creature is closest to it. If you place one in a specimen dish next to a kyrnsite, an animalculum known to propel itself by the awkward groping of its crablike claws, the paglum—though clawless—will begin moving its slender, delicate legs in a manner which evokes perfectly the clumsy, disorganized scramble of the kyrnsite. If you place that same paglum next to a feltspire, a tight little ball of a creature known for its tendency to zip quickly from one place to the next, the paglum will gently curl its body in on itself in order to appear similarly compact. And though it is not as fast as the feltspire, it will stretch its antennae in the direction opposite to the one in which it is moving, as if, propelling itself at incredible speeds, its antennae are being blown back.

During these imitations, the paglum does not alter its physical appearance radically. In fact, what is so remarkable is how subtly it is able to depict its fellow creatures. The paglum singles out defining movements, unconscious gestures. It is this sense of nuance in the paglum's mimicry that distinguishes its behavior from other creatures known to engage in similar behavior. Unlike the stick-bug or the chameleon, it is not the goal of the paglum to disguise itself. And while its impressions are uncanny, no one would ever mistake it for anything other than a paglum.

It is because its performances are never wholly convincing that they are so compelling to watch. An impressionist in a nightclub does not transform completely; such an act would be more startling than entertaining. Rather, the impressionist arranges his or her own features in a way that cleverly characterizes something essential about the impressionee. What is remarkable about this feat is that the features being used to evoke the impressionee are recognizable at all times as belonging to the impressionist. The personality of the paglum, like that of a good impressionist, remains present even as it takes on the characteristics of another creature.

The paglum seems to understand that what is pleasing about an impression is not what is included but what is deliberately left out. In other words, an impression reveals to us how much of reality can be discarded with reality still being successfully expressed. In the end, an impression is not a depiction of reality but a seeing-through, a shutting-out of everything that is not essential. In this sense, seeing the paglum do a spot-on imitation of a kyrnsite or a feltspire is rather freeing. As if you were in a nightclub, watching some desperate, ugly little man in a powder blue tuxedo flawlessly impersonate a matinee idol, you will experience a sense of exhilaration as you observe the paglum. Your first instinct will be to applaud.

— ADORNUS —

Because there is only one adornus in existence, studying it is ultimately pointless. Without the benefit of observing more than one specimen, there is no way to determine whether it is acting in a way that is natural to its kind or in a way that is specific to this adornus in particular. Certainly, it is a vibrant little creature and there is a great deal of behavior to describe, but why bother? The only thing of value that can be said is that the adornus is unique in the purest sense of the word.

By way of comparison, what we praise as uniqueness and individuality among human beings is, upon serious consideration, only an improvisation that exists within set parameters. And while it is possible for our improvisations to be wonderfully rich and complex, our capacity to be dissimilar from one another has definite limits.

What's more, in order for a person to be recognized as being an individual, that person has to have a great deal in common with the group that he or she is attempting to be distinguished from. This may seem counterintuitive, but consider the words *hot* and *cold* in relation to one another. Both are adjectives referring to extreme temperatures. The reason that we recognize these words as being opposite of one another is that, except for one distinction, their meaning is identical. Likewise, in order for a person to stand out as an individual that person must first adhere to an untold number of social conventions. If anyone were to be purely unique, that person's existence would no longer make sense to us.

That is why studying the adornus is useless. If there is no context to judge its behavior against, no conventions for it to adhere to or reject, then it is impossible for anything it does to have meaning.

— PERIGITE —

The large green rings that circle the earth are still a relatively new development, but it is already difficult to imagine the sky without them. Those two broad rings that intersect one another like the gimbals of a gyroscope are now as commonplace a sight overhead as a flight of birds. Already forgotten is the widespread anxiety that occurred when those rings first appeared—a strange, claustrophobic feeling as the once wide-open sky was suddenly imposed upon by those immense swaths of green. The initial sense the rings provoked was that the living world was being hemmed in. Now, of course, we know the exact opposite to be true.

Unlike the rings of cosmic dust that circle the gas giants of our solar system, the earth's newly formed rings are composed entirely of small creatures called perigites. These are the first organisms known to migrate successfully outside of the earth's atmosphere. So while the impression one first had was of the living world being closed off, it is now understood that these large bands are a sign that life has begun to expand out into the universe.

The common reaction to this fact was excitement. It was, after all, a triumph for the race of the living. The perigite had learned to thrive in a new medium just as our predecessors had risen up out of the sea and learned to live on dry land. Life, it was generally agreed, was marching forward, was preparing itself to populate the universe with its creative might.

However, within this celebratory mood, it was difficult to deny the simultaneous realization that, in this next glorious stage of life, mankind was being left behind. As earth's dominant species, we had up until that point assumed that life's potential for progress rested on our shoulders. But once the nature of the perigite was understood, it became quite clear that this potential rested elsewhere.

Just as we tend to look back with pity and condescension on all the creatures that are still bound to the ocean, we as a people began to understand that the next stage of life would look back in the same way on us, still bound to this floating palace of dirt.

That is why, though the sight of those rings is quite common, many still tend to regard them curiously. Naturally, as a species, our thoughts are conflicted. On one hand, we feel usurped and irrelevant. Excluded and jealous. Yet, we also cannot help but maintain that first touch of pride we experienced upon learning of life's great journey out into the universe. Despite ourselves, we regard those far-off rings affectionately. We wish them well.

— SONITUM —

Because it is transparent, the sonitum is more easily observed after being treated with a staining compound. Though, in a pinch, some diluted India ink or a drop of red wine will suffice. Also, one must remember when examining the sonitum that it is always important to shout. This creature is peculiar in that it is known to increase in size when confronted with noise. Depending on the loudness of a particular noise, a sonitum is able to swell over four thousand times its original size, making it, once stained and shouted at, visible to the naked eye. Of course, sitting hunched over your worktable and screaming at a small dish can be slightly awkward, that is, if you were driven into the field of science, as so many young people have been, by a crushing lack of self-confidence and a fear of raising your voice. However, it is crucial, in the spirit of earnest inquiry, to relax, to let your inhibitions fall slack. If you did use red wine to stain the specimen, perhaps have a glass yourself. Roll up your sleeves and shout. No reason to feel foolish.

Then again, you should also be careful not to overdo it. Sonita are remarkably elastic, but have also been known to burst. Shouting louder and louder may afford you a better look at the creature, but it is just as likely to blow the poor thing up, spattering your smock with staining compound or a limp spray of ruptured tissue. Certainly, there have been records of sonita swelling to the size of apricots after being fastened to incredibly long poles and held out into the middle of stampedes or floated out on rafts into the middle of naval battles, but these instances are as rare as their circumstances are extreme. No, it is best not to get too ambitious. Just shout at a comfortable volume and observe the fundamentals of this extraordinary creature.

For the purposes of experimentation, samples of sonita can be found practically anywhere. Sonita often hang in the air. In the atmosphere, they are known to adjust themselves with their constant expansions and contractions to the collective noise of the world. In fact, that the air around us is filled with sonita may give credibility to the long-held superstition that bird flight is a direct result of birdsong, that in addition to the pleasant chirpings and coos with which a bird at rest is accustomed to entertain itself, a bird is able to throw out its voice at such high, inaudible frequencies as to inflate the sonita in the air around it, causing the air to press firmly against the bird from all sides and allowing it to slip through the sky rapidly, like a bar of soap squeezed in a bather's hands. This is a theory of flight which is currently in vogue among the scientific community and, in an effort to support it, many have begun conducting studies regarding the vertical leap of opera singers—studies which, although compelling, are also entirely inconclusive.

The presence of sonita in the air has also been used to explain why the sky often seems to become more oppressive during a thunderstorm—why such a storm seems to constrict the observer's chest, providing a feeling of helplessness and doom—the notion being that the movement of the sonita caused by the noise of the storm forces the air against one's chest. Speculation of this sort, regarding the movement of air by means of sonita, goes on to suggest that this type of motion may be responsible for our very ability to draw breath. While it has always been assumed that the sound of our breath was the result of our breath, contemporary findings suggest that the reverse might actually be true. It is currently being argued that our lungs, by emitting the sound of a breath, are agitating the sonita around us in such a way as to drive air into our lungs. Furthermore, there are those who argue that sonita, having been thus absorbed along with that air, settle in our chests, where they constrict and loosen in keeping with the pumping sound produced by our hearts, thereby causing our hearts to pump. Pursuing this line of thought, a fascinating picture of the world is created, in which all movement and activity are impelled by their sound. This theory then suggests that any movement that seems active on our part is actually a passive reaction to the forces of surrounding sonita. And so the human body, once thought to be capable of so many awesome feats, when viewed in this light is simply an ataxic mass, only capable of producing the small ticks and groans that stir the air around it and give it the illusion of having the power to stand, to scratch its head, to lean over a specimen dish and shout.

Directed outward, this vision of the sonitic world reminds one vaguely of that much-speculated music of the universe— the consonance of all those heavenly orbs, a sound so constant it cannot be discerned. It was an idea that seemed plausible long ago, and which, in the consideration of sonita, seems even more plausible today. However, rather than that sound being a product of those movements, we may now see that those movements are the product of that sound—that the sun might very well be the product of some cosmic din so violent that one shudders to imagine it, or that the moon manages to hover above us by the grace of some cool, sweet music. It would be easy to expand upon this line of speculation for-ever. After all, human thought is not unlike sonita in the sense that, once agitated, it grows and grows. Stirred by discourse, thought begins to swell and adjust itself until the universe seems not big enough for it, until everywhere it is bumping into edges, until it seems important that it not get any larger and all the while it continues to swell and swell and swell. Though, inevitably, the source of its agitation will exhaust itself and in the terrible silence that follows thought will sud-denly contract, shrinking back down to nothing. There is, in point of fact, much research being done to suggest that human thought *is* the product of sonitic movement. Though, whether or not this supposition is valid remains uncertain. It is a complicated subject, and by exploring it here one runs the risk of overwhelming you. Remember that all this information is, for the moment, only peripheral to your task of observing this single sonitum.

Can you see it yet, in the dish? Keep shouting.

ACKNOWLEDGEMENTS

I would like to thank my amazing and unsinkable family: Mimi, Theo, Lexi, Stacie, Matt, LJ, Tori, Max, Grace, James, and Quinn. I would also like to thank Brent Van Horne for his friendship, fiction, and pathological generosity. Brent read many different versions of this book so that others wouldn't have to. Thanks to my friends and teachers Michael Czyzniejewski and Karen Craigo for their early and enduring support; thanks also to Megan Ayers, Byron Kanoti, Matt McBride, Brandi Strickland, Derek Van Horne, and Emily Wunderlich. Thanks to the following writers and magazine editors: Jordan Bass, JT Barbarese, Marie-Helene Bertino, Josh Goldfaden, Eli Horowitz, Cheston Knapp, David Lynn, Pei-Ling Lue, Alex Moshakis, Ben Percy, Speer Morgan, Arianna Reiche, Evelyn Somers, Rob Spillman, Jodee Stanley, Hannah Tinti, and Charles Yu. More teachers: Mrs. Studer, Mr. Horn, Dr. Pfundstein, and Dr. Peek. I would like to thank my fearless agent, Renee Zuckerbrot, who agreed to represent a debut short story collection during the worst financial crisis since the Great Depression. Thanks to everyone at Counterpoint/Soft Skull for believing in this project. Special thanks to Denise Oswald for all the faith and hard work that she put into the book; Dan Smetanka, who stepped in at the last minute, provided thoughtful editorial suggestions, and shepherded the collection through its final stages; Jack Shoemaker for making this all possible; and April Wolfe for being the book's guardian angel.

© Sheilah Grogan

Seth Fried is 28 years-old. His short stories have appeared in numerous publications, including *Tin House*, *One Story*, *McSweeney's Quarterly Concern*, *The Kenyon Review*, *The Missouri Review*, and *Vice*. He has also been anthologized in *The Better of McSweeney's, Volume 2* and *The Pushcart Prize XXXV: The Best of the Small Presses*.

You can follow him at www.sethfried.com.